RAVAGE MC #7

BOUND
by
desire

bound #2

WALL STREET JOURNAL & USA TODAY BESTSELLING AUTHOR

RYAN MICHELE

1st edition published: June 20, 2017

2nd edition published: September 7, 2022 — Reformatted

ASIN: B06XSDRFF1

ISBN-13: 978-1-951708-11-5

CONTENTS

RAVAGE MC FAMILY TREE

1. Ravage Me
2. Seduce Me
3. Consume Me
4. Inflame Me
5. Captivate Me
6. Bound by Family
7. Bound by Desire
8. Bound by Vengeance
9. Bound by Affliction
10. Bound by Destiny
11. Bound by Wreckage
12. Connected in Pain
13. Fueled in Fire
14. Sealed in Strength
15. Connected in Code
16. Bound by Consequences
17. Bound by Redemption
18. Bound by Fate
19. Bound by Temptation

COMPANION BOOKS

POPS & MA

CRUZ & PRINCESS
COOPER & BRISTYL & RYKER
AUSTYN
NOX & CARSYN

GT & ANGEL
DEKE & RYLIE
EMERY & JACKS

DAGGER & MEARNA
TUG & BLAZE
MICAH & ENSLEY
TANNER
RHYS & TANNER
RYLYNN
MAZIE

BREAKER & SHAINA
BUZZ & BELLA
BOOKER
AXTON
RAIDEN
GREEN & LEAH
DRYERSON & KATIE

PRINCESS — RAVAGE — Ryan Michele

RAVAGE — SEDUCE ME — Ryan Michele — GT

RAVAGE — CONSUME — Ryan Michele

RAVAGE — INFLAME ME — Ryan Michele

RAVAGE — CAPTIVATE ME — Ryan Michele

BOUND BY FAMILY — Ryan Michele
BOUND BY VENGEANCE — Ryan Michele
BOUND BY WRECKAGE — Ryan Michele
BOUND BY DESIRE — Ryan Michele
BOUND BY DESTINY — Ryan Michele
BOUND BY CONSEQUENCES — Ryan Michele
BOUND BY REDEMPTION — Ryan Michele
BOUND BY AFFLICTION — Ryan Michele
BOUND BY FATE — Ryan Michele
BOUND BY TEMPTATION — Ryan Michele

BLURB

Have you ever wanted something so badly it consumes you?

There is a fine line between needs and wants.

Deke Gavelson has wanted his Ravage cut for as long as he can remember. He's earned it. He was born to be in this club. He's not afraid to fight for his place, either.

Then she barreled into his world, and Deke suddenly desires something more than his rag and winning the next round.

Rylie Hollister has lived through hell and back. Each event makes her the strong, independent woman she is today. Until a bitter underground fighter threatens to turn her plans upside down.

These two are bound by their desires, but oh, how that changes when his intensity meets her passion.

** Bound by Desire (Ravage MC Bound Series #2) is a standalone full-length novel. You do not have to read the Bound by Family or the Ravage MC series to follow this book, but if you'd like to see the whole picture, you really should. **

To Agent K.
Thank you for always standing by me, supporting me and
being my rock.
Love you now and forever.

CHAPTER ONE
Deke

Sweat.

Heat.

Adrenaline.

The noise in the background comes through in a hushed rush as my mind zeroes in on the battle at hand.

The fist swings toward me with a powerful momentum, only missing my face by an inch. With a reflexive uppercut and using his downward momentum, I hit, and the man falls hard onto the canvas, dazed for a moment. That's his second mistake.

The first: getting in the cage with me.

Before he can get his equilibrium back, I'm on him, flipping him over and straddling his chest with enough weight to keep him down. I connect my fist repeatedly with his face, which he tries to shield with his arms. I just maneuver around him. Each move he has, I counter.

Quick and precise.

Adrenaline pumps through my veins as the roar of the crowd only gets louder.

The man's blood coats my tape-covered hands as I make contact with his eyes, his lip, and his nose. Over and over, I pound away.

There are no rules.

There are no time-outs like the big boys get. No, this is down and dirty, no holds barred fighting. Only way I'm stopping is if the fucker passes out, taps out, or is dead. I don't give a shit which way it happens. All that matters is that it will happen with me taking the win.

My chest is tight, my breathing steady, and my mind is clear. This is what I crave. What I need.

He tries to maneuver his legs to wrap around my neck, but fails because he's not fast enough. For that, I pound him several times in the temple.

Once his head begins to bounce, the "ref," as we call him, taps the asshole out now that he's unconscious. Only then do I rise, but not before spitting on the man at my feet. Motherfucker had a hard-on to get in the cage with me for weeks. Now that he's had his chance, his boys can pick up his sorry ass off the mat.

"Winner is ... Mastermind!" The ref calls out my fight name as the spectators go wild.

I'm not into that hands in the air bullshit some of these fuckers do. No, I'm more of a give me my fucking money so I can get laid man.

I walk to the entrance of the cage, and Ray opens the door for me.

"Fuck yeah," he says as I step out, handing me a bottle of water and a rag to wipe off the blood and sweat coating my face.

"Blonde," I order as if the world is my motherfucking McDonald's and a woman is just a value meal number. They all are. Holes to sink into to find release. They want to be that, I'll treat them like it.

The massive crowd parts as I walk through, no doubt remembering the last time a fucker patted me on the back after a win. His hand ended up broken. He's lucky I left it attached to his body.

Ray falls in step behind me, no doubt grabbing a woman as we move. After a fight, my cock is rock-hard and in need of the release I just gave my mind to the battle. The women around here all want it. If I looked any one of them in the eye, they'd be putty in my hands. It's the thrill of fucking someone who walked out of the cage. They're adrenaline junkies, and their rush is putting out. There's no time for games for them or myself. After a fight, I like to fuck and get out.

I bang on the rickety old door and open it, not

waiting. Ricko moves away from the window, where he watched me win the fight. He does this every single time I'm in the cage, his eagle eyes on me.

"Deacon, nice."

I'm not here for chitchat. I'm here to get paid. "Money."

He pushes away from the window and moves around to the desk. "Always a man of few words." He pulls out an envelope from the drawer, holding it out to me.

I take it, open it, and count the bills quickly, then turn toward the door, needing nothing more from him.

One thing I give the man credit for is that he pays me damn well to show up here and kick some ass. It's a bonus because needing to pound something into the ground is what I crave and what keeps my demons at bay.

"Deacon," he calls out.

I halt my steps, but that's all he's getting. Turning around isn't happening. He's had enough of my attention as it is. Never said I actually liked the guy.

"This Saturday, I have a big one for you. We'll have to travel, but it'll be worth it."

"No." I move out of the office, noting Ray standing there with a blonde. She's pretty in that big hair, makeup, and skirt barely covering her ass way. She'll do. "Come."

The clatter of heels on the tile floor are behind me. I've never understood why a woman would wear fucking high heels to an underground fight. The mass of people is so fucking thick she's bound to fall on her ass. Not to mention half the fucking floor is dirt, but what-the-fuck-ever.

I open the door to the bathroom. "Wait," I tell Ray.

"Fuck you," he retorts, handing me a condom before I slam the door in his face.

I'm not big into people watching me. Exhibitionism isn't my thing.

"Hi. You're sexy," the blonde says, trying to be sultry. I don't need seduction. We're here for one reason and one reason only. If she didn't want it, she wouldn't be here. I don't need to woo her, and she damn sure doesn't need to do anything for me but take my cock until I can shoot my load.

"Turn around, hands to the wall, ass in the air." I toss the envelope of money to the floor, pull out my cock, before opening the wrapper and slipping the rubber on it.

She watches me, and when I raise my brow, she gets with the program, turning. Then I lift her skirt above her hips.

Fucking her is like fucking all the others after a fight—a release. No woman I fuck after a fight is anything but.

She lets out breathy gasps like she's really turned on, but I've been with enough women to know she's faking. Her pussy isn't even that wet as I stroke in and out of her.

I spit down on my cock to get it lubed. Chick's so fucking dry the condom's lube isn't cutting it. It's her fucking loss. She doesn't want to get off, that's on her.

As I find my release, she lets out another groan like she's finding hers. All lies. I learned a long damn time ago about lies and the shit mess they can get you into. It's why I'm in control. Always in fucking control.

I pull my cock out and slap her on the ass. "Go."

She looks over her shoulder, pretending to be breathless, but her eyes don't even show a hint of sexual pleasure. No doubt she'll be out there, telling her bitch friends how amazing it was for her. More lies upon lies.

"You sure? I could go another round."

"Out," I order, pulling off the condom and tying the end of it. Even though my cock is still hard, it found its release and is done. Done with the fight, done with her, done being in this place.

"You don't have to be a dick," she spouts, pulling down her skirt. The tap of her heels annoys the shit out of me.

"Yeah, I do. Now get the fuck out." I wouldn't want anyone to have the misconception that I'm anything but an asshole.

I move over to the toilet and drop the condom in it, then give it a flush, making sure the fucker goes down.

She huffs, but opens the door and leaves. The entire thing is an act. One I've seen on replay every damn time I win a fight.

I'm right behind her after picking up my cash, wanting to get home and in the fucking shower.

"That was fast," Ray jokes.

I look at him like he has two heads. "One more word, and I'll bust your fucking nose," I warn, not feeling his humor one bit tonight.

"What crawled up your ass?" he asks as he walks next to me through the narrow halls.

It's strange that I can't wait to get in the cage, but once it's over, I can't wait to get the fuck out. It's like I need to breathe again, and getting away is the only way to do that.

Everything inside me is so heavy. The fight gets it all out. The weight lifts, and I need to be free, even if the moment I finish it all begins to build again.

Over and over, it's all the same. Regardless, it's how I cope.

We walk through the maze and up a flight of stairs into the dark night. When Ricko says underground fighting, he fucking means under the ground.

As we walk, I strip the tape from my hands and toss it to the dirt. My knuckles are red, but they aren't torn to hell and will be fine.

Ray and I move to my black Ford F350 and get in. I stash the cash in the center console where my handgun lays. Never know who's lurking.

While I know how to deal with my hands, sometimes that just isn't enough. And I've made enough people bleed over the past four years that someone is bound to be out for revenge at some point. I don't take chances because it's the pussies who try to jump you outside the cage, thinking they can get one up on you.

No one will get one up on me. Life lessons learned the hard fucking way: keep yourself on top, in charge, and never be reckless, but rather ruthless.

"You gettin' tired of it?" Ray asks. I know he's just trying to be a good guy, but I'm not a good man, so there's no need for him to try.

I grip the wheel and pull out into the dark night. "No."

At this point, the rush has become my drug of choice.

At this point, the battle has become my drug of choice.

At this point, the power play has become my drug of choice.

Fuck the heroin I got hooked on as a kid. The high of knocking someone out is the best kind. The roar of the crowd and the money on top, it adds to the elation, the soar, the power. All of it is an addicting concoction.

It only lasts a few minutes, but it's just enough to sate me. It's also enough to keep the demons at bay. That's the only reason I need it.

"Then, what is it?"

"Shit on my mind."

"Care to tell me?" Ray asks, sounding a bit exasperated.

"No." It's harsh, but my shit is my shit. I don't go around spreading it to others. The more people who don't know my business, the better.

Even though I've known Ray since I came to Grayson, he knows nothing of my past, unless it's hearsay from others. People talk. I'm far from a stupid man, and my last name connects all the dots. The mistakes in my life have taught me well, and there have been plenty of those. I don't make the same mistakes twice.

"Fuck, man, how am I supposed to help if you don't tell me what's goin' on?" he asks as I drive through the dark night and stop at his place.

"Out," I order.

He shakes his head. "You need me, I'm here." With that, he opens the door and exits.

I watch until he's in the door before taking off. Ray is a little dude, and no doubt he hangs out with me for protection. It's a mutual thing. He uses me for that, and I use him as my guy outside the cage. It works.

He has my back as best he can, and I have his.

My mind rolls as I make my way home. Pulling into my drive, I turn off the truck and get out. The shower is calling my name.

My place isn't the best, but it's better than sleeping on the streets, which I did for six months before finding this place.

Taking out my gun and slipping a duffle bag behind my seat, I make my way through the darkness.

I walk up the stairs to the second level of an old garage my landlord keeps his classic car in. Opening the door, I let out a sigh and lock it. The place is one open room with a small bathroom off to the side. The small kitchenette is all I need, and my bed is my couch. It works, and it's cheap. Not that I'm hurting for money. No, I just save that shit.

When I first left, I would long for the ease of crawling into my childhood bed without a care in the fucking world. Street life is the school of hard knocks. I learned my lessons well. Stuff is just stuff, and it's all just a shit reminder of what you lose when you bail. I know the loss deep in the pit of my stomach. I won't be in that situation again, either.

Control.

My surroundings are my making—bare fucking minimum. Nothing to find comfort in, nothing to miss later.

An uneasy feeling has come over me the last couple of days, and I can't figure out what the fuck it is.

My life is established. I have a damn good job, and fighting is my release. There should be nothing that would cause this unusual creep inside of me. I don't fucking like it one bit.

I head to the bathroom, strip, and wash the shit from the night off me. With my head under the spray, the water cascades down my face, pushing my hair into my eyes. The warmth doesn't help much to clear my head.

I don't like feeling unsettled. Having worked damn hard to stay in control, this feeling is foreign to me. I need to figure out what this is and deal with it. And soon.

"Deacon, my man," Cory greets, holding out his fist.

I bump it then move to set my cooler down on the workstation. I've worked at Jerry's Garage for a couple of years now. One thing I enjoy is working on cars and bikes. Luckily, I'm damn good at it. So good I've moved up to master mechanic at the shop and have been one for a year now.

It also means I'm in charge of the guys, which doesn't bother me. One thing I got down pat is an intimidating presence. The guys listen for the most part, which makes my job damn easy. When they don't, I deal.

"What's on the schedule this morning?" I ask Cory as a few more of the guys come in. I give them fist bumps as they walk past.

"Harley. The dipshit who owns it decided to change the turn signals himself to some flame looking aftermarket shit. Only, he cut his brake lines when trying to sort the wiring. Don't ask me how he did it, but he did it."

"Why would anyone customize a base model sportster? Most people consider this a chick bike or beginner's ride," I ask more to myself.

He huffs, shrugging his shoulders. "Hell if I know, man, but it's a day of rewiring for you."

He runs down the list of vehicles in line for the day, while my mind keeps going back to the Harley. My father taught me about bikes as soon as I could fucking walk. I've ridden for as long as I can remember. Mostly out back of the Ravage MC Clubhouse on a trail the guys made.

My gut twists at the thought of home. Well, it's not home anymore, and I've fucked up too badly to even go back. Not that I want to.

"You're just going to walk away?" my father growls menacingly enough that shivers go down my spine. At eighteen, he can still terrify me at times. "This is your family, and you're just leaving?"

He doesn't understand. He can't because he doesn't have a clue, and I'm not going to explain it to him. There's no point. The outcome will still be the same.

"I have to, Dad. It's the only way I'm gonna stay clean." *I keep my voice firm, steady. The drugs are a poison I can't have in my veins again. I need to stay away from the toxic shit. That's the truth, and really, this is all my father needs to know.*

I stay here, I stay on the dope. I stay on the dope, I'm going to die. There's no coming back from death. Whether he can see it or hear it, I can't get wrapped up in it. I know what the fuck I have to do.

The door was open for him to listen. I opened myself and tried to tell him. All he could see were the bloodshot eyes and the shakes as my body detoxed once again. He didn't want to hear what I had to say. There was no choice. There is no choice.

"Why? Here, your family can support you."

I want to mock him. I want to tell him that's not what he said before. I don't.

He stands to his full height with his arms across his chest. Even though I've been training with my aunt, Princess, I don't think I could take him on yet. More so, I don't want to. He's had too much anger inside of him for me for the past few years that it'll all explode. Some of it, I deserve. Others, I don't.

"I get that, but I need to do this on my own. I'm not the man I need to be, to be part of this club." *It kills me to say* those words, but it's the truth. All I've ever wanted was to become a member of the Ravage MC. It's all I thought about since I can remember. But acting like a punk kid and doing stupid shit isn't going to get me in the brothers' good graces. Not only that, but staying will only cause the brothers more trouble. It's not worth it. It doesn't matter what I want in life, this club isn't in my cards.

And they all talk about family. Well, this is the best thing I can do for my family. Whether they can see it or not, I'm no good here.

"I'm going." I mimic his stance, trying to let him know I'm not backing down from this. Also trying to convey I'm not scared, when in fact, I am a bit. Too many variables are at play right now. I just have to get past my father, then the rest will fall into place.

"You're gonna do this to your mother? Your sister? Your fuckin' family?"

I wish he could see, but he's blinded by family obligation, loyalty, and a father's love.

"It's not about Mom, you, or Emery. It's about me. I gotta get strong for me."

God, this kills. Never in my life have I wanted something so badly than to get the approval of my father. This right here will sever any chances I have of that. Ever. There's no going back and mending fences. It'll be better for all of us in the long run.

"You gotta get strong? You damn near broke us, and you

gotta leave for you?" He points to the door. *"Get the fuck out of here and don't come back until you man the fuck up."*

I left that day and never went back. Left the only family I've ever known, came here, and built my own. I may not be the man they want me to be, but I'll damn sure be the man *I* want to be.

CHAPTER TWO
Rylie

THE SOUND OF FLESH HITTING FLESH PERMEATES THE AIR, saturating it, riling it, feeding it. The vision of blood only makes the way too pumped up crowd even more crazed. The electricity in the room is like a lightning bolt, ready to sting at any given moment. The confined space of the rundown basement in the warehouse adds to the heat factor.

Every bit of this a combination for trouble. Major trouble.

Men and women hold money in their hands, waving it high in the air, each one wanting a win on the man they chose. Bets have to be placed before the first fist is thrown, so this is just grandstanding, reminding the fighters there is a prize to be won and only one of them will come out on top.

The crammed group pushes their way closer,

everyone wanting as much of the action as possible, wanting to see every cut or possible bruise. They suck in each strike, grunt, and movement each man makes in the makeshift ring.

The entire space smells of sweat and blood. The excitement in the air blends with it, making for an intoxicating experience for everyone.

One that I love to get lost in. One that not only feeds these people but feeds me, as well.

My skin prickles with each rumble as it syncs with each blow. While everyone's eyes are on the action, mine is on them. Scanning. Targeting. Watching. Waiting.

There's a moment during every fight, a peak one would say, where someone watching gets the idea they can swing like the men in the ring. Normally, it's a push or a shove the wrong way that sends everything into a tailspin.

My job is to keep that from happening. Easy? Fuck no.

A rush like no one has ever known? Hell yes.

In my three years of doing this, I can count on one hand the nights there was nothing to break up. Those three times, I almost thought of starting something just to get a rise, to see some sort of action.

I don't do boring. Refraining is very hard, but I'm paid to keep things in line, not add to the chaos. The pay is so damn good that I need for nothing. So, no way I'll fuck up this job. I know what you're thinking: why in the fuck does an underground fight need security? Schade, my boss, claims the violence, chaos, and the potential injuries are bad for business. He's all about the money and been doing this longer than me, so I roll with it.

"Rylie!" The deep voice somehow carries over the roar, and I turn toward it. Becks, another of the team, lifts his chin, telling me he's got a live one.

Finally.

My blood pumps as the adrenaline pushes its way to the surface.

Weeding through the crowd, hands touch my body, but are ignored, at least for now as the warm bodies bump against me.

Making my way over to Becks, he's in the middle of what we call a Douchebag Dance—two men who are trying to prove how big their balls are. Average sized men, both taller than me, and each has between fifty to a hundred pounds on me, as well. One is dressed like he just came from some type of office job with a navy Polo shirt and dark jeans. His build isn't enormous, but he's not lacking, either.

The other is a regular, Jackson. Of the hundreds of altercations I've broken up, he's been in several of them. He came from the streets and is a hell of a scrapper. In his late twenties, he loves the pain and gets off on it. Even a punch and he's happy. One of these days, I'm going to throw his ass in the ring and let one of the guys show him real pain. Or just do it myself. That's where he needs to be instead of throwing his weight around out here.

Jackson rears back his arm for a punch. Before he can do so, though, I loop my arm through his crooked one and twist it behind his back, at the same time kicking his kneecaps and causing him to fall harshly to the partially concreted and dirt floor.

With his arm locked and me slightly bent, he can't move, and with the serious blow to his kneecaps, he's down for a bit. Pity.

Becks rushes Polo man and has his ass down on the floor, too.

The people around us move just enough to give us space, but still staying in the action of the featured fight. They couldn't care less about this one. Now, if the main event was over, this would be an entirely different animal.

Polo man looks shocked that his ass is lying in the filth. This makes me smile. Stupid fucker.

"Out," Becks calls over the rumble, picking Polo man up to his feet and escorting him from the room.

I tug on Jackson's bent arm, and he yelps. "Up," I command, knowing full well that he won't be able to walk smoothly out of here. But there is no way in fuck I'm carrying his ass out. Not that I couldn't. I'll just leave it to the cleanup crew. Schade doesn't fuck around with his job. Therefore, neither do any of us.

Speaking of cleanup crew, Turner shows up, an angry scowl on his face that I'm pretty sure is permanently etched there, considering that, for as long as I've been here, he's never once smiled.

He says nothing, just grabs Jackson by the arm and neck, dragging him through the crowd.

Well, that was uneventful. What a fucking let down.

The loud bell chimes, signaling not only the end of the match and someone completely down and out, but also ringing in my fucking ear. Schade insisted on the fucking thing. Why? I have no clue. It was put in about two years ago when he got a wild burr up his ass, and to my regret, it hasn't disappeared.

Hands from the audience fly down as the sound grows more intense. Some are pissed they lost their cash, while others are brimming with excitement.

Becks catches my vision, lifts his chin, and moves through the crowd, same as me, scanning and watching.

A body crashes into my back, making me stumble forward, but not enough for me to go down. Turning, I see a man with brown hair look back at me for just a second before he turns back toward another man who is charging at him. Arms swing, punches connect, grunts sound, and blood sprays the surrounding crowd that has now turned to these two, their cheering and egging on now going to them.

This is exactly what I was talking about earlier. Now that the real fight is over, the attendees are ready for more blood, and they don't give a shit whose it is.

This is more like it.

Moving quickly between them, I slam hard into the man's kneecap, and he goes down with a *thud*.

Yes, I have a lady boner for kneecaps. They always take a person down if you hit the right spot.

The other man takes a swing at the same time, hitting me square in the jaw. I can feel my bright red lipstick smear across my chin as the pain shoots up the side of my face. My head doesn't turn, though, making the man who hit me take a step back and blink rapidly, the shock quite funny.

I step toward him and look up since he has a good five inches on me, even in my heeled boots. With a speed I've honed in on, I let my fists fly in rapid succession. Up, across, and even to his nose, as he bends a bit because of the blow to his stomach. Blood spurts out, spraying me. But I don't give a shit, in this moment.

He puts his hands up to deflect. A couple of times, he even tries to punch back but only hits air as I maneuver away from each strike, getting mine in, in the process. Savagely, I strike him in the gut with my boot, making sure the pointed heel takes the brunt of the contact, and the man falls to the ground, smacking his head and passing out cold.

Damn, it was just getting to the good part.

"Fucking bitch!" is yelled behind me, and I turn to see the man who I dropped out of the fight early. He's holding his knee, pain written all over his face. I take simple joy in that, even if his mouth is spouting off stupid shit.

"Aw, you say such sweet things," I coo before slamming my fist in his face.

Looking around at the crowd, I first check to see if anyone else is in the mood to bombard me. Not seeing any takers, I inhale a breath, letting the high take me over. It's better than any fucking drug out there, and one I can ride until the next fight.

Life has been a challenge. One I refuse to lose. So, bring it on, motherfuckers. That's how I get through every night at this job.

"I SWEAR, you get off on this more than anyone," Schade comments, handing me my envelope of cash after the night is over. Not only do I get a cut of the winnings, I also get my pay.

Schade doesn't fuck around. When he hired me, he

said that it was because I was the best. I don't know if that's true, but I do what I do and that's the end of it.

"Someone's gotta do it," I reply, placing the envelope in my black backpack then zipping it up. I throw it on my back, adjusting the straps before making a quick exit.

My bike hums between my thighs as I cruise down the dimly lit streets. The cool night air whips across my face, invigorating me. I've always loved riding, ever since I was a kid. Then, money was scarce. Hell, more like non-existent, but we made due, like always.

I would watch the motorcycles go up and down my street, always dreaming that one day I would own one. Now, the Harley is mine. I've worked damn hard for it, but I learned from my parents' that anything worth having is worth working damn hard for. Having taken that to heart, my entire life has been about just that.

The air against my skin, the sounds all around me, and the experience of flying down the wide-open road reminds me that I'm alive. Cars, trucks, SUVs, they're all nice, but being caged in makes me feel suffocated. Riding on the open road, the power of the machine between my legs, it's a reminder I'm a damn survivor.

Pulling into my driveway, I scan the place, looking for anything out of place, noting nothing out of the ordinary. The bricks on the house are exactly the same, landscaping the same, and the one light in the living room glows through the window. Nothing amiss. The same as always.

I hit the button on my bike and the garage door rolls open. I park the Harley next to my silver Jeep. Climbing off the bike, I unzip my leather jacket and pull my clear glasses from my eyes as I walk to the door.

Beeping comes from the other side as I slip through and enter the code for the alarm. Just then, paw steps are heard running through the house. The taps of Brewer's nails hit the hardwood floor and skid as he turns the corner.

I kneel as he barrels into me, almost knocking me down. He's a sixty-five-pound black lab with a ton of energy, and I love him. He's my solid in a world of liquid.

He gives me his doggies kisses as I rub him down. When I rise, he whines, then gets excited when he sees me moving toward the kitchen. He loves dinner time. Or, in our house, midnight dinner on days I have to work. He goes to town as I toss my backpack and everything else down on the table.

When I moved to Sumner, Georgia, it was because of this job. A friend of mine said he knew a guy—when you're deep in the streets, connections are everywhere. It looked interesting, so I thought I'd give it a shot. Now I've been here for three years.

My house is simple: kitchen, attached dining room,

living room, three bedrooms, and two bathrooms. The furniture is the same—I only have what I need. Nothing fluffy, no throw pillows or decorative vases with flowers in them. None of that shit. Everything in my space serves a purpose. The extras mean nothing to me.

Thanks to Schade, I can afford pretty much anything, but why throw money away on stupid shit? No thanks. That's not for me. The only luxury I have is my bed. King-sized, extra comfy, with blankets I can melt into. My reasoning for this is a bit twisted, but when you grow up too fast, too soon, too unprepared, you learn quickly the things that make you happy. My bed is one of those. Brewer is the other.

I strip off my clothes, tossing them to the floor, and jump in the shower. After washing off the night, I climb into bed just as Brewer hops up, turns twice, and finds his doggie place beside me. I drift off.

"WHAT?" My tone is clipped and irritated, because I am irritated. As soon as I saw Aunt CB—CB stands for "cunt bitch"—it shot my day all to hell, and I've only been up long enough to eat and let Brewer out. Nowhere near enough time to deal with her.

If I didn't answer, though, she will just call and call

and call to the point where I want to reach through the phone and rip her head off.

"That's no way to answer the phone, Rylie. Have you no manners?"

"No," I answer instantly, having lost manners a long damn time ago when it comes to her. The only reason I deal with her is because she's the only family I have left, being my mother's sister and all. I've felt stuck for a very long time because she's the only connection I have to my parents'. But that's about to stop because she only calls for one reason and one reason only.

I'm not a fucking ATM machine, and my mother's sister or not, I'm done.

"I see." She clucks her tongue, the same fucking sound she made when I was a teen and did something she didn't approve of. Fucking hated that shit. She would do it right before punishing me for stupid shit, like asking for a second helping at dinner time. I learned quickly not to do that.

She is nothing like my mother. Nothing. My mother was warm and caring, while CB is nothing of the sort.

"What do you want?" I ask again, grabbing my Diet Coke and taking a drink then sitting it back on the side table.

Brewer comes up and lays in the crook of my bent knees on the couch.

I know what she wants, so why the fuck do I even ask?

"I'm a little short this month—"

"No," I cut her off with a quickness. "I'm not giving you anything. Only fucking time you call me is for money and to get you out of some fucked up situation that you got your own damn self into. I'm done with this fucking game. You need to lose my number."

She huffs. "Rylie Marie—"

"No," I cut her off again. "I'm not fucking paying for your shit. You're lucky your ass is still breathing. Take this for the warning it is: leave me the fuck alone, or I'll make you ... for good." I disconnect and toss my phone to the other end of my couch.

That bitch just does not know who she's fucking with. I'm not some punk-ass kid who lost her parents in a drive-by shooting anymore. Living on the streets was better than her home. I've learned my shit and have a damn good head on my shoulders, no thanks to her.

Thank Christ I only had to stay with her for two years. Worst two years of my life, but they made me the woman I am today. Not that I'd ever thank her for that ... ever.

CHAPTER THREE
Deke

I ROLL OUT OF BED, BRUSH MY TEETH, AND TURN ON THE coffee. Every day, it's the same routine.

Set.

Predictable.

Controlled.

Steady.

My phone rings, and when I look at the screen, I see, *Emery calling*.

I feel my lips tip into a tight smile. My sister, who's away at college for her first year, is the only one I've kept in contact with from home. Emery is a light that I sure as hell don't deserve, but take anyway.

I swipe it and accept the call, just like I always do.

I'll never leave her hanging. No matter how fucked up my choices in the past, she's always accepted me as I am with open arms. When I couldn't look in the damn mirror at myself, she loved me the same. Nothing ever changed between us.

She was only fifteen when I left home and still innocent to so much in life. Even when I was fucked up on dope, she was always on my radar. I made sure she was okay. There is nothing I won't do to keep my sister safe.

When I made the decision to leave, it killed me to leave her, knowing I was abandoning her in a way. Knowing that, when I left that house, her life would be forever changed. But in the end, it was best for all of us. Even then, I'll do anything in my power to protect her.

"Yeah?"

She lets out a huff. "You could at least say hello."

"No."

"Nice to talk to you, too, asshole." I hear her moving on the other end, like she's rolling on a bed or something. Then another huff comes over the line.

Not that I intend on being a dick, it's just who I am now. She knows this. She accepts it.

"Talk, Emery." When the coffee pot beeps, I pour myself a cup, then sit on the bench at my small table.

"I'm dropping out of school," she lays out on me like a bomb exploding.

She's too damn smart to just give up. And one thing Emery isn't is a quitter. She doesn't give up on shit easily. Hell, as many times as our conversations ended up only being a few words, she still puts up with my ass. There's no way that after our parents forced it down her that she was going to college she'd just drop out. She's never been one to disappoint our parents. Nothing about this is in Emery's usual nature. There must be something else going on.

Time to get to the truth of the matter. "The fuck you are. What's the problem?"

"Wow, you can actually speak sentences. Good job." She's always been a smartass. It shouldn't make me happy to hear it, but it does. Even under these circumstances, she reminds me at times that I do give a shit. At least with what happens in her life.

"Emery ..." I warn, a billion and one things going through my head. Is she hurt? I'll gut the bastards. Is she pregnant? Again, I'll gut the bastard.

"Fine. I suck at this. The classes are super hard, and I'm getting bad grades in two of the classes." She sighs between her rambling. "Mom and Dad are going to flip their shit when they find out. I just don't think this is for me."

I'm sure her classes are hard compared to high school, but she can hack it. She's been on the honor roll more times than I remember. Besides, everything in life is hard; it's what you do with it that matters. Choices are hard, and this one doesn't need to be rash.

I play it easy.

"Alright."

"Alright? Did you really just say *alright* to me,

Deacon Alexander?" she yells into the line, shocked by my answer. Good, that's what I was aiming for.

"Yeah, you wanna quit and be a quitter, that's on your shoulders."

"Quitter? I am not a quitter!" she shouts across the line, and I try not to chuckle. She's too easy.

"Yep, givin' up your first year without givin' it a shot. So, what now? You're goin' home? You gonna work at X, too?"

X is a strip club the Ravage MC owns. My aunt Princess runs the place, but there is no way in hell she'd hire Emery. Still, I need to get a rise out of her.

"I don't know what I'm doing." Something crashes on the other side of the line.

One thing that runs in our family is our temper. My father has a hell of one. Me, I take mine out in the cage. Emery, she hasn't exactly figured out her way yet. Except for throwing things, that is. Even after four years, she's still the same.

"But you're quittin' school." The statement is meant to be harsh, and she obviously takes it that way.

"What, like you quitting the family?" she charges back, giving it to me tenfold. Not much hits me or gets me down anymore. Those words, though, strike a direct hit.

"Didn't quit ..." My words trail off because, in a way, I did, not that I had a fuck of a lot of choice.

"Coulda fooled me. You haven't even been back for Christmas. Christmas, Deke? I mean, really?"

Setting my cup down on the table, I rest my elbows on it, looking down at the chipped wood. Darkness fills me. It eats at me and claws its way to the surface. I try to push it down, but it does no good. Instead, it festers.

Emery has no fucking clue. None. She has no goddamned idea what I gave up for her, our parents, and the fucking MC that I was never good enough to be a part of. Every damn want I had in my life, I tossed to the side ... for them. Fuck, I shouldn't even care anymore, but when she says shit like that, it cuts deep.

Instead of continuing the path of this conversation, I change it. "So, you quittin' school or what?"

"Like you give a shit," she grumbles, and I lose it.

They can all think what the fuck they want about me, but not her. Anyone can say I'm a bastard, a dick, or a fuckwad, but for my sister to question my concern, my care, or my fucking loyalty ... it's a time bomb about to blow.

"Yeah, I do give a fuckin' shit! You're too goddamned smart to drop out. You keep your ass there, get that fucking piece of paper, and make something of your damn self, Emery. You don't need Mom, Dad, me, or that club. You can do it all your fuckin' self."

She sniffles over the phone. Fuck, I hate when I make her cry, but she needs someone to knock some damn sense into her.

I take a calming breath. Even when she was a baby, I could never stand to see her cry. It's not in my makeup or something. I've never wanted Emery to feel a single ounce of pain. This shit she's spewing about dropping out of school, well, as much as this conversation hurts her now, it's going to be worth it when she gets through.

I drop the animosity in my tone and make sure to give my sister the comfort she needs. "Emery, you're smart and have a great head on your shoulders—use it. Dropping out isn't an option, so suck it up and deal. You need a fuckin' tutor to help you, tell me and I'll send you the money for it. You need help from a teacher, I'll do that, too. But you're not quittin' and goin' home."

"Deke ..." she whispers in my ear with a crack in her voice. "I don't know anyone here, which means, if I'm not at class, I'm in my dorm room. My roommate and I don't get along, and I just hate it here." At least I'm getting down to the nitty-gritty of the problem —friends.

"Isn't Micah there with you?" Micah is Tug and Blaze's son. Tug is a brother in the Ravage MC, and Blaze is his ol' lady. Micha is the same age as Emery. Hell, I think Emery picked this school to go with Micah and not be alone.

It's no secret that my sister has had a crush on him since she could walk. Lucky for Micah, he hasn't shown any interest in her that way. Otherwise, I'd have to pound his ass into the ground. Still, Micah is Emery's family. My sister should not feel alone when she has family.

"I'm not talking about him." She huffs in a way that tells me not all is well in their little world. Tough shit. Life sucks.

"What." It's not a question; it's more of a demand for her to talk.

A long pause comes over the line, and I hear her sniffle again.

"He has a girlfriend."

Hell, didn't exactly see that one coming. Back when I was home, Micah never kept his head out of a damn video game long enough to notice my sister was even there. He used to run into fucking walls because of it. Not to mention he made it clear he hated the club. That did not sit well with anyone.

Born Ravage, die Ravage, that is something you don't question. Micah, though, he just didn't seem fazed in the slightest by the club life. While guys like Cooper, me, and even Nox made plans in our heads about what it would be like to have our cuts, Micah only seemed to care about the next level on his game. His future was never about Ravage, even if it was in his blood.

"His loss."

She hiccups. Damn, she needs to call Austyn, our cousin, for this girl shit. I am not cut out for it.

"Emery, you need to meet some friends to hang out with. There has to be a chick in one of your classes that you can start talking to." Listen to me giving my sister advice on how to make friends. Regardless, she's the one damn person on this planet I'd do anything for. Even go up and pound Micah's damn face in for being an idiot.

"It just sucks."

I have no doubt that it does, considering she's been surrounded by her family for her entire life. And I'm not talking me and our parents. No, I'm talking about the entire Ravage MC and their kids. There was always someone around to hang out with. You never had to be alone, unless you wanted to. Especially the girls. They were kept in a protective bubble of a sort, yet taught how to handle themselves. Meeting new people is out of her comfort zone.

If I closed my eyes right now, I could go back in time to when it was easy. I won't, but I could.

Growing up there started off well, but it didn't end that way for me. My choices came with deep consequences, the life altering kind. For Emery, it's a huge adjustment that she needs to suck up and get used it to. Her strength will sustain her. It's one of the reasons my parents wanted her to go away to school. They wanted her to be independent and able to take care of herself. I can see that. Now, she just needs to deal.

"Yep, but you've got this, Emery. I have every bit of faith in you." I mean every fucking word of it, too. I believe in my sister. She has smarts, strength, and loyalty. She can get through this and come out better on the other side.

"Thank you," she says softly. "I want to see you, Deke."

Four years of only talking on the phone, and she says the same thing during every conversation. As much as it guts me, I can't. I can't go back there. None of them understand, and I'm not about to explain it.

"Someday," I say, giving her the response I always do.

"Yeah, someday. Bye, Deke." She hangs up before I can say bye, and an ache in my chest forms. Tossing the phone to the table with a clatter, I run my hands through my hair.

Even if I could go back, being the man I am today, my father wouldn't accept me. Not only did I leave abruptly, but even before that, I wasn't good enough.

"You need to get your shit together," my father says, *standing in the doorway to my bedroom. He's been on my ass lately because of my report card. I only got one F. It's not like they were all that way. Hell, I even got an A in class of them so that balances shit out.*

"It's good, Dad."

His face grows stern, not angry, but in the way his cheekbones protrude and his eyes get focused. This always leads to bad shit.

"Good?" *He steps into the room and closes the door.* "You call getting a fucking F in Science good?"

"It's only been a quarter. I'll bring it up."

"Yeah, you fuckin' will bring it up. Until then, your ass is grounded to this room and chores whenever your mom or I say so."

This isn't a surprise. Doesn't mean I'll stay in my room, either. I've become the master of getting out of this room.

"Fine."

"I should smack some fuckin' sense into ya," *he grumbles, leaving.* "Gonna be the one who tests us all," *he mutters on the way down the hall.*

It's not until much later that I open the door to my room and listen, thinking everyone is asleep. How wrong I am.

"What are we going to do?" *my mother asks in a soft voice.*

"Fuck, I don't know. That boy's goin' down the wrong path. It's mostly teenage shit, but the grades and dickin' off at school ... Beatin' him isn't gonna work."

"No, you are not beating our son," *my mother says, and I smile. She always defends me on pretty much everything.*

"Wish he grew up to be more like Cooper. Have his head on straight and have some damn direction. He's not gonna make it. Why can't he just follow the path Cooper did? As much time as they used to spend together, thought for sure* *he'd be alright. It's a shame." My father's words make the pit of my stomach fall out as the ground beneath me disappears.*

I'm not good enough.

I'm a fuck up.

He wishes I was like Cooper, not me.

My father would be shocked as hell to find out the man I've become over the last four years. Not just Deacon Alexander Gavelson, master mechanic, but Mastermind, the hold nothing back fighter with balls of fucking steel. Too bad he'll never see it.

He'll never know the strength it took inside me to walk away and not come back. He'll never know the broken pieces lost long before I ever had my first high. He's never going to know a damn thing about me and the man I've become.

Feeling the need to pound on something, I head to the gym.

CHAPTER FOUR
Rylie

"MOTHERFUCKER," CHARLIE SPOUTS OFF AS HE LIES ON the floor from the kick to the gut I just gave him.

I try hard not to laugh, but a smile still tugs at my lips.

I've fought since I can remember. My parents used to call me a scrapper. I laugh inside at the thought. If they could only see me now. It was bad before. Then their deaths only pushed me more. Things just got worse when I lived with Cunt Bitch, taking it to a fever pitch. Or maybe better, considering my skills have improved. Guess it's the way you look at it.

"Now I bet you're pissed you trained me so well," I chide, holding out my hand. He takes it, and I help him to his feet.

"If I weren't so fuckin' proud of you, I'd be pissed."

He slaps me on the back as we make our way over to the bench in the gym and take a seat.

I did set him down pretty hard, and he is getting older. Not that he's out of shape. He's more on the stocky side, but with a lot of muscle. His hair is more salt than pepper, but he's still got the moves.

He's been training me since I landed my ass here. I actually found him because of Schade. Somehow, we just clicked.

"Right." With a roll of my eyes, I grab the water bottle and down half of it as sweat pours from my body. Workouts with Charlie always end up with me drenched. I wouldn't have it any other way.

"Surprised you're not workin' tonight."

"Tomorrow. Supposedly, some hotshot is coming in, so we have to be on the up and up."

Schade always pays well, but when a big fighter comes to town, he pays better. That's because the guy usually has boys who come with him. Those boys usually start something, or one of our regulars starts something with them. Newbies don't get the welcome carpet.

If they make Schade money, though, he doesn't give a fuck who goes in the ring. Me, I find it quite entertaining.

"Nice. Maybe I'll come check it out." He shrugs like it won't throw a fuck of a wrench in my work.

"Nah, I'll be too focused on keepin' your ass safe. Can't do my job."

"Me safe?" His hand flies to his chest. "Sweetheart, if you can tell by the ring, I can hold my own."

Inside, I smile. "Know that. Just don't want any distractions. Pulls me off my game."

He chuckles then downs his water. "Your game is fine."

"Whatever."

Charlie is going to do what he wants, so I let it go. There's no reason to argue with him.

"You wanna come over for dinner tonight?"

"Can't tonight. I'm goin' out with some of the girls."

His brow quirks. "You actually have girlfriends?"

I bump his shoulder. "Shut it, ol' man."

"Who're you callin' old?" He chuckles.

Most men would have their pride hit from the barb, but not Charlie. He's man enough to roll with it, and that's what I like about him. He's a calm in the storm I call life. When I needed coping skills, Charlie took me in the ring, in the cage, and move by move, he gave me strength and control at a time when everything was spinning like a tornado.

"Skyler, Breelyn, and Avery are meeting me. We need to cut loose for a while. Too much testosterone everywhere."

"You feed off that shit, so don't give me that."

It's true, so I just chuckle in response.

He smiles, his eyes softening. "Good to see you goin' out."

He leaves out the "after you caught that dickhead cheating on you," but he doesn't need to say the words because I know. Hell, I almost went to jail for sending his balls into his throat and showing the bitch riding him how I solve things. Luckily, Schade has connections in the police department.

It gutted me at the time, thinking there was something wrong with me. That I wasn't enough for a man. Then I got wiser. He's not man enough for me if he pulled a pussy move like that. Fuck him and the horse he rode in on.

Lance should have been smarter, but he wasn't, so he paid the price. I'd be surprised if he can have children now. I should get a fucking award for that one. No one needs to have him procreate.

"Yep, I'm good, Charlie. Really. I'm not pining over him or wishing on a star that he comes back to me. Or any of that fairy-tale bullshit. I'm happy he's gone and took his trash with him. Still, it's good to go out."

It's been weeks since I have gone out. Work and training keep me busy. And the girls have lives of their own, too, so finding a time when we could all get together wasn't manageable until tonight.

"Good. Now get out of here," he orders, pointing to the locker room door.

I laugh, shaking my head as I rise. I have a night to get ready for.

"SHOTS!" Skylar shouts over the rumble of music booming out of the speakers in the space. Bimbos' is a laid-back bar that we enjoy spending time in now and again. There really aren't a whole lot of choices in Sumner, and we normally don't want to go outside the city.

Men and women shake and shimmy on the dance floor, hands in the air with hoot and hollers. Others sit at their tables, nursing whatever concoction they have in front of them. Us, we're just getting started.

The waitress comes by, looking at all our faces and plastering a smile on hers. I'm nowhere near as intoxicated as my friends. Drinking isn't a big thing for me, but being with my friends is. Letting loose for some people is getting inebriated. Me, not so much. I like to keep my attention on everything around me. Some habits don't die.

"Tequila!" Skyler calls out as Breelyn hits the table several times in quick succession before throwing her hands up in the air with a cheer. Avery rolls her eyes, but she has a large smile on her face.

My girls. The four of us have been friends since I

moved to Sumner. Breelyn works the front door of Schade's place, taking the cover charge fee for all the people who want to watch. Avery and Skyler oversee the fighters, making sure they have what they need. Schade doesn't fuck around.

I sip on my beer as the waitress leaves.

"I started dating a guy—Brody. He's super cute," Skyler starts with a smile gracing her lips. This doesn't surprise me one bit. She always has someone she's dating or has dated at some point. She has serious daddy issues. We leave her be so she can carve out her own path. For the most part.

Staring into her eyes, I see something is missing. Yes, she's happy with him, but he's lacking somewhere or their relationship isn't what she wants.

"And ...?" I ask.

She sighs heavily and looks me dead in the eye. "He's a good boy." Her tone is so down, a laugh escapes my lips.

"Like 'em bad, do ya?" I tease.

"Who doesn't?" Breelyn pipes in. "Tattoos, muscles ... hell, maybe even rides a Harley. What's not to like?"

"It's just ... I don't feel the spark. I like him, but not in the throw-me-against-the-wall-and-fuck-me way. I want that. Someone who can't get enough of me and who I can't get enough of. Someone who, when I walk into a room, his eyes are only on me."

While I wish her luck in this, it doesn't exist. Some

may call me cynical. I don't give a fuck. All those pipe dreams of ever finding a man to do that for me went out the window a long damn time ago. There is no fairy-tale happily ever after shit. It's all made up.

"Yeah." Breelyn sighs dramatically while Avery looks to the dance floor.

"Nah, who needs all that? Find you a hottie to go home with tonight and have fun. You only get one life. Live it up and don't try to push things." My reasoning sucks, but I've never said I'm an expert.

"Yeah," Breelyn responds as the waitress comes by and drops off the drinks. We toss them back as a familiar song comes over the stereo system. Breelyn's eyes light up. "Come on!" She jumps up so fast there's a slight sway to her step, but she recovers quickly.

"Hell yes!"

We all make our way to the dance floor, moving to the music, letting it carry us away. Bodies press into us, but we remain next to each other, dancing our asses off.

Letting loose isn't something I normally do, because doing that means you aren't in control of your surroundings. I like to know what's going on and who's where. But dancing is an outlet for me. Some may say that my outlet is fighting and beating people up. It's not. That's my job. Not the beating people up part, but it seems to come along with the territory. It doesn't make me feel free, though.

Dancing, getting lost in the music, the heat surrounding me, that does.

I make the most of each move and get lost in letting the rhythm take me away. By the time we're done, sweat glistens off my body and my breaths are difficult.

Falling back into my chair, I suck in the much-needed cool air.

"Damn, that was fun," Avery says, pulling up the chair next to me. "Did you see that guy trying to dance with you?"

I look toward the dance floor and spot him instantly. Since I kept brushing him off, I hope he got the hint.

"Not my type."

"What is your type?" Avery challenges, lifting her hand to the waitress.

"Fuck if I know anymore." I thought what Lance and I had was something special. He comes to the fights, which is where we met. He was persistent, and my dumbass gave in. We were together five months, and the fucker cheated.

"You need a man."

"I need my vibrator. Men are a pain in the ass that I don't want to deal with."

Breelyn stumbles up to the table with a wide smile, Skyler right behind her. "Let's go to X!"

X is a strip club here in Sumner, owned by the Ravage MC and run by Princess, an ol' lady in the club.

You'd have to live under a rock ten feet underground to not know this information in this town. It's also hot and a whole lot of fun.

"Hell yeah."

We pile out of Bimbos' and head to X. I'm happy the last thing I drank was a glass of water and not the shots Avery wanted since I'm driving. If I couldn't, I wouldn't get behind a wheel.

We make our way up to the front door of the strip club where a large man sits. As soon as he sees us, his arm goes out, ushering us through. One good thing is they never make women pay the cover. They know, as well as we do, the men will all be looking, and not just at the women on the stage.

Breelyn makes her way through the crowd, everyone filing behind her, as we find a table in the front. More like, there were two men sitting there, they saw us, and got up quickly, then two more chairs mysteriously showed up so we each could sit. Funny how that works.

The woman on the stage sways her hips seductively to the music, like she's been doing this for years. Her long, dark hair has an edgy feel by the way she flips it, bringing on the seductive look. The black leather puts up a don't-fuck-with-me vibe, adding to the men around her going crazy. She owns the stage. It's admirable, the fact she can get up there, dance in front of all these men, and have such confidence in doing it.

I'm not sure I could. It takes a special kind of confidence to pull that off.

Pulling out dollar bills and passing them to the dancers, we make sure each of the girls are tipped well as we laugh, drink, and enjoy ourselves, picking up some moves along the way. We're standing up by the stage, dancing, interacting with the woman on stage who is eating it up because the guys are all over it and money is pouring on the stage.

Two men come up behind Avery and Breelyn, grinding against their asses. We're all dancing. I think nothing of it until Breelyn's gaze darts to mine with panic written over it. Halting and taking in the situation, I see the man's hands are roughly grabbing Breelyn's ass as she turns around repeatedly, telling him to stop and trying to pull away from him. He holds on tight with his other hand, not letting her move.

Bastard.

Marching up to him, I push him off her. "She fucking said no!" I yell over the music.

He glares at me after bumping into a table where several guys are sitting. Each one of them rises, trying not to let the spilled beer get on their clean dress pants. They need a new hangout if they want to be so damn clean.

"Bitch!" he growls, coming toward me.

Fuck yeah, this is what I'm talking about.

He charges. Two shots to the face has him

stumbling backward. A swipe of his feet has him falling flat to the ground on his ass. Then my hair is pulled from behind.

What the hell is it with men and pulling a woman's hair? That shit needs to stay in the bedroom.

Lifting my leg, I nail him in the gut, and he doubles over.

"Bag!" I call out to any of the girls.

Avery tosses my bag to me. Quickly, I grab the zip ties, just as guy number one comes at me. I just step out of the way.

His momentum is so much that he doesn't stop, causing him to fall on top of guy number two, who yells at him to get off.

Not wasting a second, I pull guy one's arms behind his back and secure them, pressing him into guy two to hold them both down.

I look around for a damn security guard. They've been everywhere all night, yet the one time I need them, they're nowhere to be found.

My friends surround me.

"Are you okay?" Skyler asks as I blow a loose strand of hair away from my face.

"Peachy. Can you find a guard or someone?"

Just then, a bulky man who looks as though he's a brick house pushes his way through the throng of men. He looks at me, then the men, and back at me.

"What the fuck is goin' on here?" his deep voice bellows.

"Playin' Candy Land," I clip, wanting very badly to roll my eyes.

He crosses his arms over his chest.

I huff. "Fucker wouldn't keep his hands to himself. Thought this place was supposed to be good on security?" People talk, so I know X has the best, or so I thought.

"And you did all this yourself?"

"What the fuck!" A woman's voice comes from my left.

I turn my head, meeting *the* Princess. She's hard not to miss with her dark hair with bright red streaks in it. I've seen her out and about in town, but have never officially met her. Only heard of her. And what I've heard is she's pretty fucking kickass.

The guys below me start to move more. It becomes a struggle to hold them, so I let them go, but stand at the ready.

"Fuckers can't keep their hands to themselves," I tell her, and her eyes narrow at the men. With one in zip ties and two a bit dazed, it's almost funny.

"Dammit," she growls, turning to the bulky man. "I told you to keep an eye on them." This comes as a shock, but I listen. "You knew them dancin' up there would be a magnet." She doesn't yell, but her tone is not mistaken. Deadly. Fierce. Powerful.

"I was—"

"Don't," she growls, clenching her fists. "No excuses. Go see Cali and get reassigned."

He starts to talk, but one look from her and he decides to just leave.

"You two, don't fuckin' move," she orders.

The guys halt as she pulls out her phone and sends a text to someone, then looks back at us. It's strange being in this woman's presence. She's had such a reputation in the community for so long that she almost seems like an illusion. Not really here. Almost like a celebrity that you occasionally see on TV, but don't really get the full effect. Being this close, I can feel the anger coming off her. She's definitely here.

"Sorry about that. These assholes will be dealt with." She nods toward the men.

"Appreciate it."

"Did you do that yourself?" she asks.

"Hell yeah, she did. She's the best!" Skyler says, and Princess' brow raises in question.

"It's my job."

She goes to ask me something, but stops as two men barrel up to us, eyes pissed as hell. But fuck me, they're hot. One has tons of tattoos, while the other only has a few. They are both well over six feet tall. One has light brown hair that's tied in a knot at the back of his head. The other is dark-haired with a playful yet sinister look on his face. They wear the

Ravage MC logo on their leather. Great, now they're involved.

"These two," Princess says.

Without a word, the Ravage MC guys grab the assholes and guide them out of the place.

"Your job?" she asks, not missing a beat.

"I work for Schade."

Her eyes narrow to slits. "Rylie?"

This shocks me, and not much does these days. I've been there and done that for a long-ass time. Her knowing my name is strange.

"Yeah."

A smile graces her face as I cross my arms over my chest. "No wonder you could put these two out. I've heard about you." She shakes my hand. "You just made a friend."

I smirk. *Friend* is a relative word, but I roll with it. Who doesn't need someone like Princess on their side?

CHAPTER FIVE
Deke

"TONIGHT. NINE-THIRTY," RICKO SAYS IN MY EAR AS I SIT at my desk in the shop. Jerry, the owner, said I needed one to make sure the right parts were ordered, even though he knows I give all the orders to the secretary and she enters them in the main office. As long as the job gets done, he's happy.

It is nice to get away in my own space, though.

Ricko's call comes at the perfect time. I can feel it building. The need for release. The need for escape. The drive that can push me over the edge if I'm not careful. I've felt pent-up since the call with Emery two days ago.

It doesn't do anyone any good to play the woulda, coulda, shoulda game. That's not in the cards. The present is all one can deal with, but that doesn't stop the worry I have for her. I refuse to let her go down the wrong path like I did. Not that she's to that point, but I've been texting her to make sure her head is still on straight. So far, she seems to be pulling herself together, but I may need to suck it up and make a trip to her school. Seeing her won't change anything, but maybe it'll help her in some way.

A throat clearing brings me back to the conversation on the line. "How much?"

"Seven K."

Sure, the man is out to make money, but I need to make this shit worthwhile.

"Ricko," I warn, not about to say more. He'll pay. He always does.

"Fine. Ten K, but that's all I've got for this one."

It's funny. That's exactly what he says at every fight. I'm not stupid. I do my homework. The assholes who come to these fights have serious cash and bet it like it's water. Knew one guy who walked out with thirty thousand, just on bets. High rollers with money to burn. Therefore, I know Ricko pulls in serious cash.

"I'll be there." I click the phone off, tossing it to the desk. At least tonight I'll be able to let go of the build inside.

Take that, demons, I tell myself before pushing out of my chair and getting back to the shop where I can put my mind and my hands to work.

LIKE ALL THE others after a fight, the drive home is quiet after dropping Ray off at his place. The guy tonight got in a few good shots, but nothing I couldn't handle. I relish the pain. It's a reminder I can still feel, that I'm still alive.

When I left the cage, he was passed out on the mat. With each punch I threw, a small bit of weight left my shoulders, but unfortunately, not enough. Even the fuck after didn't release anything this time. If anything, the weight felt a bit heavier.

Darkness surrounds me as I pull into my place, seeing a figure sitting on the steps leading up to my apartment. They're hunched over, a hoodie covering them, their arms wrapped around their knees. It appears like they are rocking back and forth.

Whoever it is, they are obviously here for me. No one should be here, especially not for me. No attachments.

I pull into my spot and park. With my gun at the ready, I exit the truck.

When the figure rises, I lift my gun, pointing it right at their head.

"Deke, thank God."

I remember that voice.

"Austyn?"

She pulls the hood away from her face, and her dark hair falls, reminding me of Aunt Princess. Shit, she's a spitting image of her—hair, body, and even some of her facial features. Even in the dark of night, she stands out like her mother.

"Hey, how's it goin'?" she asks as if we haven't seen each other in four years and this is just a causal meeting.

I lower the gun and holster it behind my back. The closer I get, the more I can see her face. I don't fucking like what I see. The left side of her face has a huge bruise on it, and her eye is swollen.

"What the fuck happened?" I ask, getting closer and examining her face.

She takes a step back, no doubt realizing I'm not the kid I once was. My body is bulky yet lean. Not to mention I've been told by Ray that I look like I can break a man in half. I could.

"Upstairs, then you talk." I point.

With a large exhalation of breath, she turns and moves up the stairs.

I move around and unlock the door. She steps in, and I flip on the switch as she looks around the place. In the light, I can see the many shades of purples and greens as the bruising is no doubt setting in. This is recent. I don't like it even more.

"Nice place?" It comes out more of a question, but I don't give a fuck what she thinks of the place. The only way she could've found out where I live is if Emery told her. No one else knows. Well, the club keeping tabs on me could be a possibility. With the way things were left between my father and I, however, I don't think that's the case.

"Cut the shit. What happened?" I toss my shit to the small table then turn to look at my cousin. She's grown up a fucking lot. No doubt Aunt Princess and Uncle Cruz have their hands full, and that's by looks alone. The fire in her eyes adds an entirely different dynamic that no doubt will go *boom* at some point.

"I just need a break from home. I talked to Emery; she told me to come here."

"Austyn, I don't do bullshit. Fuckin' talk or leave." Not that I'd truly let her leave with a busted face in a place she doesn't know, but she doesn't need to know that. In fact, when she gets her shit sorted and out of here, it's best she not know the hold the family still has on my heart, my loyalty, and my mind.

Her eyes don't meet mine as she speaks. It puts me on edge. "I got into a little bit of trouble."

I step into Austyn's space, and she takes a step back, bumping into the wall. Her breaths pick up, and a small bit of fear flashes in her eyes. Good.

Her eyes lower a bit. "Please step back," she requests quietly, and after a moment, I do. "I left with this guy I met at party. He took me on a bit of a road trip." She's being vague, so I cross my arms over my chest and clear my throat. "Alright, we skipped town. I wasn't planning on being gone long, but it's been a couple of days. We got into a fight." She lifts her hand up to her face. "And he kicked me out of the car."

"And you just happened to get kicked out at my doorstep?"

"No." She looks away. "I hitchhiked here."

"You what!" My words are explosive. I want to beat some ever-loving sense into her brain. "You fucking hitchhiked? Have you lost your goddamned mind?"

She holds her hand up, trying to placate me, but that's not happening. "I made it here, that's all that matters." Her voice cracks. There is more to this story. She's avoiding my eyes. Austyn is shaken, but why?

Anger bubbles in my veins. Has she not learned anything from anyone?

"That's not all that matters. Fucking hell, Austyn! So many things could've happened."

She runs her fingers through her hair, pulling it at the roots. "You think I don't know that? I couldn't call Mom, Dad, Cooper, or Nox."

"Why the fuck not!" I'm fully aware that I'm arguing with my twenty-year-old cousin, but I don't give a fuck.

Austyn has support. She has family. It's not that I'm not willing to pound the fucker in the ground for her, because I am. Why come to me when there is a clubhouse full of badass motherfuckers ready to pounce in the name of family?

"Look at my face, Deke!" She points to it. "If they find out about this, I'm fucking toast."

"More like he's toast," I growl.

"No, Deke." She moves into the space, making small passes. "Things are different now. So much different." She shakes her head.

Things aren't that different. Emery shares enough; I would know if Austyn had a reason to worry about going home.

"I'm sure they are, but they sure as shit are looking for your ass right now."

"I texted Nox and told him I was fine, that I'd be home soon."

"Give me your phone."

She reaches in the back pocket of her jeans, pulling it out. "It's dead."

I don't answer. Instead, I tear the sparkle infested cover off, then the back of the phone. Pulling out the battery, sure as shit, there's a chip in it.

"Fuck," I growl.

"What?"

"You can't be this stupid, Austyn."

Her hand goes to her hip, and in that moment, the look on her face is just like my aunt's. Fuck, that's freaky.

When no one would listen, when I couldn't stop

the rattling in my head, Aunt Princess was there. She didn't force me to talk. I asked her to teach me to fight, to give me the escape, the control, and she did.

"I know there's a tracking device on it. That's why I let it run out before I got close to your place so they wouldn't know where to find me. This is the last place they'd look."

Fuck, that guts, but it's no more than I should expect.

"I can't let them see my face. All of them will go apeshit, and I'm already in deep with Mom and Dad."

"You're fucking twenty-years-old, Austyn; why haven't you grown the fuck up?" I bark.

"Oh, I have in more fucking ways than one, so don't you sit there and lecture me on that shit, Deacon! None of it's your goddamned business!" She sucks in air. "Look, I just need a place to crash for a couple of days while my face heals, then I'll go home and face the music."

"And you think you're staying here? With me?" I open my arms, gesturing at the tight space. "No, you're going the fuck home."

"Deke ..."

"Not tonight. You sleep on the fucking floor, and I'll figure out what to do with you tomorrow. Need to shower." I turn.

"Why are you all busted up? Your face and

knuckles look like you've been fighting," she asks, studying me for the first time since she got here.

I don't turn. "It's what I do." Then, rather than explain, I shower.

I knew that if I told her I was taking her ass home right now, she would bolt when I got in the shower. Therefore, I lied. Once I get this fight off me, I'm driving her ass back to Sumner. The damn place I never thought I'd go back to.

Fucking hell.

The water does nothing to tame the beast inside me. Going back is a really bad idea. It could do so much fucking damage, but I can't let her stay here, and no way in hell am I calling Nox to come get her. They don't know where I've been, and they don't need to know. I'll take her there, drop her off, then get the fuck out.

The problem is, when I get out of the bathroom, she's passed out, asleep on my couch. And fuck, it looks like she hasn't slept or eaten in days. I'll let her sleep, feed her, then take her home.

Yes, I can give her the night, but tomorrow, she goes home, and so do I.

CHAPTER SIX
Rylie

MY CELL RINGS THE NEXT MORNING. LOOKING AT THE screen, I see it says unknown caller. Swiping it, I take the call, knowing at least it's not the cunt bitch.

"Yeah?"

"Rylie?" a woman's voice comes over the phone.

I wipe the sleep from my eyes, my mind instantly connecting the voice to the person.

"Princess?"

She chuckles. "That obvious?"

"What's up?" This is totally strange. First, how the hell did she get my number? Second, what the hell does Princess Cruz want with me? Third, did I fuck something up last night I shouldn't have? The thoughts continue as I listen for her reply.

"You're coming to work for me." It's not a question; it's a statement.

Bolting up from the bed, the sheets fall to my waist. The sudden chilly breeze sends goose bumps on my flesh through my tank top.

"That's nice and all, but no thanks."

"Just listen for a minute."

I say nothing, giving her the cue to continue.

"My head of security at X put in his two weeks' notice about a week and a half ago. Gar, the guy who was supposed to be watching you girls, was up for the job. Last night proved he's not ready. I want you."

Not gonna lie and say I'm not good, because I am. That's why Schade pays me the way he does. It's also why I don't need another job to sustain my simple lifestyle. Another serious reason is, I'd be in the fold with the Ravage MC. Putting a big target on my back isn't really a move I want.

"Appreciate it, but it's not a good idea." Even as a rush of adrenaline fills me, I know it's best to stay away.

"Not takin' no for an answer. You can stay with Schade; we'll work around those hours. And I'll pay ya double what Schade does."

I fall back to the bed in a puff of sheets and blankets. Double? Double what Schade does? She obviously has no idea what he pays me. There's no way a strip club would want to fork out that kind of cash when they could find someone a hell of a lot cheaper than me.

"You do realize how much Schade pays me, right?"

She laughs over the line. "A fuck of a lot. That's why I know you're good. The best come at a price."

A chuckle escapes me. She's damn persistent.

"Thanks, but really, I don't need another job right now."

"Tell me what the hang up is, and I'll take care of it."

"Anyone ever tell you you're damn persistent?"

The phone moves like she switched ears. "All the time. Tell you what; meet me at the clubhouse at one. I'll pull my husband and a few others together, and we'll talk about what you need. Told you, you will work for me."

I shake my head as I look up at the ceiling. No one bosses me around. And no one puts restrictions on me. Not even Princess, the head ol' lady of the Ravage MC. Not happening.

"No thanks. I'll see ya around."

I lift the phone, just about ready to hit the end button, when she says, "I'll be at your house in twenty." Then she clicks off.

"Fuck!"

Tossing the phone to the bed, I climb out quickly and move to the bathroom. Noting the makeup still on my face from last night, I jump in the shower and clean myself off.

Princess is coming to my damn house. I didn't even know I was on her radar in the first place. All of this because of last night. One incident and now the head of the club is showing up at my doorstep to get me to change my mind. Fucking hell.

The Ravage MC is big in this town. There are so many rumors flying around about the club, though most of it is hearsay—nothing confirmed. My assumption is that's how they want it. They don't like people in their business, and I don't blame them one bit, since I don't like people in mine.

After showering, I toss on some jeans and grab a T-shirt that says "suck it." Staring at the woman in the mirror, a small smile plays on my lips. My blonde hair comes to my shoulders with the tips a cross between blue and purple. When I went to the salon, I told them I wanted fun and got this. I love it. It's different.

I chuckle just as the doorbell rings, followed by a fist pounding on the door. Alrighty then.

Another round of pounding occurs as I reach it, unlock it, and then swing it open. Princess stands there in ripped jeans and a shirt cut low on her chest. Her dark hair reflects the sunlight, not to mention the fire red streaks. She wears a smile on her face, but a sinister vibe flows from her. Not many can match me, but I'm thinking Princess could. At the same time, it doesn't intimidate me in the least. If anything, it makes me respect her even more.

"Come on in," I say, stepping back from the door and letting her enter.

My place is me. Bold colors of reds and purples accent the space while the walls are a light gray. It's not messy, but it's not picked up and tidy, either. Who has time to waste on putting shit away when you're just going to get it back out in a couple of days? My time is more important.

Princess moves into the living room, taking a moment to look at my space before her focus comes back to me. She's definitely on a mission, exuding so much confidence I'll need to keep on my toes.

"What can I do to get you to come to X?"

A chuckle escapes me as I sit in my recliner. She follows, taking a spot on the couch, never taking eye contact away. She's intense, that's for damn sure.

"Look, I appreciate you wanting me on your team, but it's not a good fit for me."

"Why?" she fires back. "Because of Ravage? Or is it because you just don't want to? Clearly, a strip club isn't an environment you dislike, since you and your friends came in to chill, so what is the problem?"

"It's because I make enough money with Schade that I don't have to. For as little time as I actually work, I don't need the cash. It would just take up my time." I shrug more to myself than her. There really isn't an issue with working in a strip club. Hell, my girls and I went there for fun; she's right about that. Money is always great, but bottom line, I don't want club shit at my door.

"Bullshit."

"You're right. It's the club. Having my ass tied to it could cause me problems, and I'm not into having problems, Princess." While rumor on the streets is the Ravage MC has cooled down quite a bit over the years, they still do what they do, and with that comes trouble. Trouble I don't need.

Her face grows hard while my body goes on red alert. I have no doubt a duel between her and I would rival any fight in the ring. She is undoubtedly used to getting what she wants.

"I'll guarantee you that nothing with the club will affect you."

I smile. "Yeah, and how does that guarantee work?"

A slow grin breaks over Princess' face, obviously thinking she's won this battle. "Easy. Club shit stays out of X. You're in X; therefore, it doesn't touch you."

"And if it does?"

"Then I have your back. The club has your back. No questions asked." She leans back against the couch. "I get it. I do. There's always a risk, but know we protect our own. Bottom line is, I have shit going down."

My head tilts in question.

"No, personal shit. I need someone I can trust to take over the security so I don't have to deal with it right now."

"And what makes you think you can trust me?"

Her eyes narrow. "You sayin' I can't?"

I meet her stare straight. "You can. But how do you know?"

"I read people. Last night, I read you. And Schade obviously trusts you. I'm kickin' my own ass for not thinkin' of you sooner."

It's interesting that she thinks so highly of me without really knowing me, but I've earned it. My time scrapping as a kid is useful for something. May not have had much, but I've always been me.

"How long?" I ask, suddenly letting this idea roll around in my mind. "How long till your guy Gar is ready to handle his shit?"

Her eyes snap to mine, surprise flitting across them, which she covers quickly. Inside, I smile at having caught her off guard. Something tells me that doesn't happen often and probably won't happen again.

"Indefinitely. You're the one for the job."

I shake my head. "No. Three months. And you gotta know, Friday and Saturday nights, I'm at Schade's."

"Three months. First four weeks, you're at X either Friday *or* Saturday night. It's our big crowd." She sits up on the couch, her attention directly on me as she clasps her hands in front of her and rests her elbows on her knees. This is negotiation Princess. Nice.

Princess is a fuck of a woman, and I can't help a

small twinge of nervousness talking to her. No way in hell I'd let it show, though.

"Three months. The first two weeks I'll be at X either Friday or Saturday night. But you have to pay me what I would have made at Schade's, plus what you're going to pay me."

She shakes her head. "I can't believe I'm fucking negotiating this shit. Fine. But after you spend those four weekends at X, we talk again and see about extending it."

Damn, she's tough, especially for something I don't need. She must really want this.

"Fine. And Princess?" She nods. "Don't fuck with my job with Schade. You talk to him and try to get me fired or my hours changed, I'm out. Automatically. That goes for you and everyone else with your club. Schade is off limits."

She full-out grins. "Knew you had a good head on your shoulders." She rises. "Follow me to the clubhouse. You can meet my ol' man and the guys. They're in and out of X, so you need to be aware of them. Not to mention they want to meet the woman I'm bending over backward to come work for me."

"Doesn't happen often, huh?" I ask as I rise.

"Fuck no. Try never. Like I said, I've got personal shit and I need someone. Let's go." She makes her way to the door as her cell rings.

I grab my keys and lock the door.

"Yeah?" I hear her as I move to my Jeep, swinging myself up and in.

"You're fuckin' shittin' me."

My focus goes to Princess, but I'm cut off from hearing any more as she slams the door on a black Hummer and powers out of my driveway. This is going to be interesting.

I've driven by this place a few times since moving here, but never actually been here. Pulling up, barbed wire lines the top of metal gates, and a guard stands on in a parapet, his hand on a gun. Mine's in my glovebox. What a way to meet your employer, but it's coming with me.

The large gates slowly slide open, revealing an enormous cement blocked building with a huge open grass area that has a fire pit in the middle and a playground off to the side. Cars line one side, while bikes line the other. Off to the right is Banner Automotive, the local repair shop. I've never brought my car here, but they must do lucrative business, judging from the movement inside the building.

I park the car then reach over to pull out my gun.

A tap on my window has me turning to the sound to see Princess standing there. I open the car door.

"Don't take guns in. My ol' man'll be pissed, and then I'd have to deal with his shit, which means you have to deal with his shit. We seriously don't want to deal with a pissed off Cruz."

I hesitate, weighing my options. I really don't have any at this point. I've already agreed to work for her, so it's not like I'm going to go in guns blazing or anything. Not to mention I have no reason to. My hands and feet can protect me plenty. They have a shit-ton of guys here, though I'm sure, if they wanted to take me out, they'd have no problem. I may be able to take on several, but all of them ... I'm not fucking Superwoman.

Releasing the buckle, I climb out of the car, taking in a deep breath. Smells of oil and fire fill my nostrils, and my first thought is: *I hope nothing's burning.* Looking around, I see nothing.

Princess begins to move, and I follow.

"Alright, Cruz knows you're comin'. We've got family shit to deal with, so this'll be short and sweet. I'll introduce you to the guys that are around. The others, you'll meet later."

I'm obviously going to be dismissed after my meeting with her husband, which is fine by me. My list for the day didn't include coming to a motorcycle club and meeting the president, let alone having his ol' lady show up at my house, offering me a job.

Whistles come from the picnic benches where several guys sit. Three to be exact.

One man is covered in tattoos. He has this vibe that screams different pussy every night. That's his view on women. Reading people in a split-second is what I do for my job, so I know I'm the prey and he's the predator, ready to eat me alive.

The middle one seems tame, not really taking me in like a meal, but rather along for the ride. It doesn't really fit the expected vibe I had for bikers. Meanwhile, the third is laidback, confident, and focused solely on me. He's reading me as hard as I'm reading him.

"Green, Jacks, and Ryker," Princess introduces. "Be nice; she's workin' at X."

The one with the tattoos stands up and saunters over to me. "Hey, baby. Workin' at X, huh? I'll give ya a ride." His cut reads Ryker.

Just catching myself from rolling my eyes, I smile as he leans in a bit, thinking he's got me. I inhale him, the smell of cigarettes coming off loud and clear. He's hot, don't get me wrong, but he's not a man I'd take home with me. Too much going on in that head of his.

I lower my voice and tell him, "You couldn't handle this ride if it came with training wheels." His eyes flair. "Not a challenge. Truth."

"Ryker, she's not dancin'; she's security. Now back off. You're gonna scare her off before I even get it all worked out."

"Nah, he doesn't scare me. It'll take a lot more than him to do that. Thanks for the vote of confidence, though."

Princess smiles. "What, Ryker? This must be a first. Nothing to say?"

"I'll have your panties by the end of the week," he declares with a grin.

"Don't hold your breath. Or, on second thought —do."

Ryker's eyes light in amusement, yet there's something behind them. It's as if he's covering for something or someone. Maybe this in-your-face shit really isn't him—it's an act. Pity. I know a lot of women who would eat that shit up if it were true.

"Come on."

I turn and follow Princess in through a large metal door. When it closes, I have to blink my eyes several times to adjust to the darkness. The place smells of smoke and stale beer, reminding me of Schade's club and my time tending bar. Damn, that feels like a long time ago.

The place is covered in a dark wood paneling that looks as though it's been there for more years than I've been alive. There's a bar off to the right with nicks and dings all over it. Tables and chairs, some filled with people, sit in the middle of the place. A large pool table sits off to the side, and there's a wall full of pictures all over it.

"Well, who do we have here?" a man with long hair braided down his back and a red, white, and blue bandana across his forehead calls out from one of the tables. He lifts a beer to his beard covered lips, takes a sip, then sets it down.

"Rylie," Princess answers for me. "Dagger, meet my new head of security at X."

He whistles. "What's a little thing like her gonna do with that job?" I'm sure he's joking, but I don't appreciate being belittled.

"Wipe the floor with any motherfucker who doesn't keep their fucking hands to themselves." My tone is calm, even, and still. Yes, I can make my voice still in a way that conveys my seriousness. I've had quite a bit of practice over the years.

Dagger takes another drink then points the tip of his bottle at me. "She'll do ... for now." He throws it down like a challenge, but I don't take the bait. It takes a lot more to hook me these days.

Now, the scary as fuck guy to his right, he might be one of the few I don't want to ever see in a dark alley. His face is twisted in a way that I think is permanent and strange. He's all muscle and can more than likely take out anybody and anything. He's definitely one for me to keep my eyes on.

"Rhys, this is Rylie."

Scary man—okay, Rhys—says nothing, but lifts his chin.

"Come on; be nice," a sing-song voice comes from beside me. A beautiful woman with blonde hair and a body to die for walks up to Rhys, making his scowl disappear as she sits on his lap, putting her arms around him. "Don't be all hard to the new girl."

He pulls her to him and kisses her hard. I hear her gasp, but she doesn't pull away. His face changes. It doesn't get soft, but there's this slight change that is tender. That man loves her beyond all reason.

"Tanner?" Princess calls out as they pull away for breath.

When she turns to us, her eyes are a bit glazed over. "Yeah?"

Princess chuckles. "This is Rylie."

"Oh, hi! Sorry." She looks at Rhys. "Okay, not really sorry, but yeah."

"Nice to meet ya," I tell her, feeling a bit flushed after witnessing that kiss. Damn, it's been a while, and seeing the passion they have for each other is a sight. Not to mention he's got a few years on her.

"Stop doin' that shit in front of me," Dagger growls.

"Dad, we're married and have kids. This shit happens all the time."

This is a shocker. So, Dagger is Tanner's father, and Rhys looks about his age. To each their own. Regardless, they're hot together, so I count her as pretty damn lucky. Not many women have what those two have. And even though I don't know her or him, I'm happy for them. Anyone who can find a slice of happy in this world deserves it.

"Hey!" A woman with long blonde hair and a wide smile comes up to Princess' side. "I'm Bristyl, Cooper's ol' lady." She holds out her hand, and when I take it, I notice instantly her strength. This woman is definitely not a push over. More so, she's Cooper, Princess, and Cruz's kid's ol' lady, and judging by the wide smile on Princess' face, this woman has her approval.

"Rylie."

Bristyl looks at Princess. "This is good. It'll give you a break."

Princess nods. "Yeah, Rylie here is solid."

"She looks it. I work here at the shop in the office. If ya need anything, let me know." She gives another wide smile before she drifts out the front door.

"There you are." That male voice is so damn deep, and the man behind it is hot as all hell.

Princess marches up to him and wraps her arms around his neck. The infamous Cruz. It's actually his last name, but it's what he answers to.

Princess stands on her tiptoes and kisses him. He pulls her in close and deepens it.

Damn, it's seriously getting hot in here. The way he kisses her reminds me of last night's conversation about getting thrown against a wall and fucked hard. This man, he definitely does that with his woman.

She pulls away. "This is Rylie."

He takes a beat to admire his wife then turns to me. His eyes and demeanor that were once happy with Princess turn cold and razor sharp. I don't move or take a step back, even if his fierceness makes me want to.

Never back down. He wants me to work for him,

then it'll work. If not, then I'm out. That's the good thing about this situation. I don't like it, I'm done. No harm, no foul.

"Let's go to my office."

"Sure."

Great, I'm off to a good start. I should just hightail it out now.

CHAPTER SEVEN
Deke

"I GOT YOUR SISTER," I SAY INTO THE PHONE AFTER NOX greets me.

"Who the fuck is this?" Nox barks from the other end of the line.

He's always been the calm one, except when it comes to his sister. He's always protected her, no matter what. I have to give him that, at least. He and I had our differences, but it's been years.

"Oh, cuz, calm your shit."

"Deke?"

"Showed up on my doorstep. Bringin' her home," I tell him.

A slight hesitation comes over the line. "Is she okay?"

"Nope. Busted face. Whoever that dickwad was she was with left her black and blue."

"Fuck!" he growls. "I'll find out who it is."

My instant reaction is: *fuck yeah, let's go beat this motherfucker down*. Then reality hits me. Drop her off and leave. That's what's best for everyone. Getting involved any more than I already am is bad news.

"Be there this afternoon." I disconnect the phone and toss it in the cup holder.

Austyn begins to move from the passenger seat of my truck, her eyes flying open. "Where are we going?" she asks in a rush.

"Home."

"You asshole! You told me I could stay with you." She moves to take her seatbelt off. I'm going about seventy, so if she goes out, she'll make a fuck of a mess of herself.

I reach over and grab her arm, tightly holding her in place. "No, I said you could stay last night. Already called Nox, and he's expecting us."

"Fuck, Deke, do you have any idea what you've done?" She fights just a bit, then groans, dropping her head onto the back window. I take it as my cue to let go. "I'm fucking dead."

"Shoulda thought of that before you hopped in a car with someone you didn't fuckin' know. That's some stupid shit right there, Austyn. Know you're smarter than that."

She sighs heavy. "Fuck, Deke, you have no idea what you've done. You have no idea what's going on."

"Fuckin' enlighten me so I know what I'm gettin' myself into." Damn, this is a horrible fucking idea.

"I lied."

I slam on the brakes and pull the truck over in a flash, my gaze shooting daggers at her as I clip, "What?"

She reaches out, putting her hands on the dashboard, bracing herself. "Don't get pissed."

"Too fuckin' late. Talk."

Her eyes fill with something, and she quickly tries to mask it, but it was there—hurt, pain, regret.

"You can't tell anyone, Deke. I'm confiding in you. I can't let anyone know why I was in Grayson."

"Talk!" I bark.

"Deke," she snips back. "I mean it. This is serious shit."

"Talk. I'll decide."

"You're not gonna let me go unless I tell you ..." Her thoughts trail off as if she's weighing what to tell me. "I didn't hitchhike. I'm not stupid. I took the Greyhound here, not wanting the tracker in my car to keep tabs on me."

"Well, at least you have some sense."

She lets out a huff. "If you'd have been around the last four years, you never would've bought the hitchhike thing in the first place." My anger rises. "I needed to do something, and it couldn't be in Sumner. Emery told me a while back where you were living, so I planned that something here so I could crash with you for a couple days."

"What something? And don't fucking blow rainbows up my ass, woman."

A small smirk tips her lips. "We've missed you."

"Austyn ..." I warn.

She lifts her chin as she straightens in her seat like she's gaining her courage. What the fuck is she up to?

She clears her throat. "Let's just say, yesterday, when I came to town, I was pregnant. Today, I'm not."

Shock hits me in the gut. This scenario wasn't even on my radar. I feel as if the wind is knocked out of me.

"What?"

Her head whips to me, tears and anger burning in her eyes. "I'm not talking about it anymore, Deke. You got more than I wanted to give."

"What about your face?"

Her fists clench. "You should see him. Fucker outside the clinic said I was a murderer. Said I didn't deserve to breathe. Said I was a whore. He came at me, and I didn't think he was actually going to hit me, but he did. I fought back, of course, but he got a couple licks in."

"So, let me get this straight; you just had a procedure, and you're out beating the ass of some asshole?"

"Yeah, Deke. That's why I passed out at your place.

They gave me some painkillers, and I took them after I got out of the cab at your place."

"Fuck, Austyn. Why didn't you tell me this yesterday instead of fuckin' lyin'?"

"No one knows I was pregnant. I mean, no one except now you. You think I want anyone in our family to find out what I did? They'll be pissed. But I couldn't keep it." Her breaths come shorter, and if I'm not mistaken, she's biting back tears. There is a far off look in her eyes.

"Who's the father?" Not only will I beat the motherfucker, but I'll make sure I pass the information on to Nox, Cooper, and Cruz so they can get their shots in, as well.

Austyn crosses her arms over her chest and faces forward. "That, I'm not discussing." Her tone is flat. I can feel her shutting down, so I change it up.

"Your brother knows you have a busted face. What are we gonna tell him?"

She slaps her hands to the side of her seat. "Fuck, Deke. They can't find out who did it. That asshole will sing like a canary and tell them the demon I am. Think, Austyn." She says the last part to herself, evidently trying to come up with another lie to cover up what she's already done.

"You know, the more lies you tell, the harder it is to cover your tracks," I tell her a lesson I learned the hard way. When it comes down to it, things were better for me to leave and stay gone than to attempt to continue the lies.

"I know that, Deke, but in this situation, I don't have a damn choice."

"You're bringing me right back into the middle of shit I can't and don't want to be in. Did you think about that?"

Her head snaps toward me like something just dawned on her. Good. Maybe the little shit can get her act together.

"Sorry." The word is so damn soft I barely hear it.

"Why did you do it?"

She lets out a small scream; the quiet gone. Then she throws her head in her hands and begins rocking back and forth. "This is why I didn't tell anyone. I don't want all these questions," she growls. "Fuck."

I don't do this deep shit. The closest I've come is with Emery and school. This situation is completely on the other side of the spectrum, and while I want to tell her to woman up and fucking deal with what she did, I can't. I may be a dick, but I'm not a complete bastard, and from her expression, this was a hard decision for her.

"You were mugged while comin' to my place to get away. I didn't know. When you got off the bus— because Austyn, they'll find that shit out—you were mugged. You kicked his ass, he got away, you came to my place."

"You think they'll buy it?"

"Nope."

She actually chuckles. "I'm so screwed, Deke."

"You pay cash for everything and not use your real name?"

"I had a fake ID, and yes, I paid cash. I'm not some stupid kid, Deke. I had it planned out to the T. One thing I wasn't planning on was the asshole coming at me and you taking me home while I'm busted up."

I need to get her home, so I steer the truck back on the road.

Whatever she decides to tell them, they will investigate and will find out the truth. It's the Ravage way. And I'm driving right toward it.

"Where am I takin' you? Your mom's?"

She shakes her head. "No, my place."

This is fucked up on so many levels, and fuck me for bringing her home. It's put me square in the middle of this mess and on my way to a place I said I wouldn't go back to. But I'm not fucking heartless, at least not most of the time.

Austyn doing this shit on her own is beyond my comprehension. The girl of four years ago is no more. I have questions for her, but I won't ask. It's not my place. After I drop her ass off, I'll be on my way. She'll go on with her life, and I'll be away from Sumner.

When my cell rings, I look at the number.

"Your brother."

She groans and lets out a scream, then grabs the phone and takes the call. "Yeah?"

It's faint, but I can hear. "*Yeah? What the fuck are you doing, Austyn? Who's the guy, and why is your face busted up?*"

She looks at me. Guess I forgot to tell her I'd already told him she was with some asshole. Lies, all they do is compound, making each heavier than the other until they collapse. When they do, it takes down everyone in their path. Me, I don't give a fuck. This isn't my business. My life is in Grayson. Not in Sumner. Never in Sumner.

"Deke misheard. I took the Greyhound up here to surprise Deke."

At least that's the truth.

"Why?"

"Because I needed to get away, Lennox. Now get off my ass!" she bites back, gripping the phone tightly. I wouldn't be surprised if I hear plastic cracking at any moment.

"You bring your ass to the clubhouse, Austyn," he fires back, all while I take in their conversation and continue to drive, knowing I've fucked up, but no way would I let Austyn fend for herself to get home.

"No, I'm going home."

"I'm not fuckin' playin'. Dad's pissed beyond measure. You don't even want to know how Cooper's taking your disappearing act. I mean, really, Austyn? Where the fuck is your brain? Takin' off without tellin' anyone where you're goin'? Then we can't track your cell. It's fucked up."

"No, I'm going home. I'm tired. I'll deal with you all later."

"If you're not here, we're comin' to you. Don't be stupid. Make the right decision."

She pulls the phone away from her ear, staring at it. "He hung up on me."

"No shit."

She huffs. "Don't add to my plate, Deke. It's deep enough without you piling more on top."

"You did this to yourself. And you'd better figure your shit out, because I sure as hell don't want to drop you off at the clubhouse, but it's your best damn bet at the moment."

"Great, gone for four years and you take their side."

I clench the wheel. "Fuck off. You think I want to go to that place? You'll be lucky if I don't push your ass out of the truck and keep driving past."

"You wouldn't." No, but she doesn't need to know that.

"Fuck yeah."

Her eyes narrow. "You're a dick. Just like all the other guys."

"You expected different? You got a lot to learn, woman." It feels different calling her a woman. She's not even legal to drink yet, but here she is, dealing with a responsibility she didn't intend on doing. All in all, she's handling herself damn well, considering the circumstances.

"Fuck, this isn't how I planned it."

"Nothing ever goes as planned. That's why you need to know every possible outcome."

"You know, Emery said you didn't talk much. I think I'd like it better if that were true." I feel the urge to chuckle, something I haven't done in a long-ass time, but I hold it in.

There's no need to respond, so I don't, just turn my attention to the road and drive. She needs time to think, and I need to prepare myself for what's about to come next.

"Deke, please," my mother pleads, tears running like rain down her cheeks. Each one that falls to the ground guts me just a bit more.

Since as long as I can remember, all I've ever wanted was to become a brother in the Ravage MC; to take a seat at their table with my father, grandfather, and uncle. Life decided to throw me a big "fuck you," though, crushing those dreams into shards.

"Mom, I have to." More like, I don't have a choice at this point.

If I even wanted to stay here, it's not an option. Nothing is an option, besides leaving. It's for the best. The brothers think I'm a joke. Hell, my own family thinks I am. What else can I expect from them after I got high to numb it all for over a year.

It was a shit move, but it's one that I have deal with. Probably for the rest of my damn life. Funny how all I ever wanted to do was grow up so I could join. Now I wish I could do it all over again. However, life doesn't work that way.

"No, you don't. Just stay, and we'll work all this out. We can't do that if you're not here," she tries again.

I lean in and kiss her cheek, inhaling the smell of sunshine she always reminds me of. "Yeah, I do. Take care."

I move away as I hear her continue to cry. My instinct is to go up to her and hug her, but it's better this way. I'm not the person she needs to have for a child. I'm not even close.

That drive away from Sumner was both hard and liberating at the same time. With each mile in my ratty old car, the more freedom I felt, and the more the anger bubbled to the surface. The anger won over, something I've lived with for four years—hell, longer, if I really think about it.

None of that matters, though. Nothing matters when it comes to the Ravage MC. They are them, and I am me. The end.

Fuck them for wanting me to be something I'm not. Fuck them for being my family in the first place. Just fuck it all.

I feel the burn deep in my belly. The churning, the

fire, the need. I fight to push the demons down. The urge will always be there in the recesses of your mind; that's what rehab taught me.

As buildings come into view, a gnawing takes hold of my gut. Familiar places of where I grew up pass by in a blur, and before I know it, I'm stopped in front of the large gate.

The guy at the top stares down at us. Austyn rolls down her window and yells up at him. Then the gate slowly opens, and my past and present collide.

Everything looks pretty much the same as the last time I was here. But I know so much is different because I am different.

People still park their cars in the same spots and bikes on the other. Not one damn thing has changed. I can't say the same for myself.

"You gonna come in?" Austyn has this hopeful gleam in her eyes, almost like she wants me to protect her from what's about to come. I'm not the guy for that.

"No. Don't come back to Grayson."

I watch as her face falls and wetness forms in her eyes that she quickly masks. Her hand trembles, and I'm positive she has no idea she's doing it.

"Please. I know I've asked a lot from you, but you're here. What kind of man does it make you to not even say hi to your own mother? You know she's here. The moment she heard your name, she rushed here."

My damn black heart squeezes, causing an ache in my chest. "Nice guilt trip."

Austyn smiles. "Whatever works. Besides, I need someone on my side."

"What makes you think I'm on yours?"

Austyn really doesn't know how lucky she has it to have a group of people at her back that would take a hit for her at any time. Those men would lay down their life for her, including the women. She has solid support, yet she's not using it. I can't help wondering why. Why is she not allowing herself to lean on them?

"Deke, just ... just please."

She's a fucking little shit.

I reluctantly open my door and hear her do the same. I inhale, noting every scent that reminds me of this place. Rubber from the tires in Banner Automotive, oil, trees, leather—it's all in the air. Many of the same smells I have back in Grayson, just without the bullshit of trying to live up to something I'm not.

"Deke," I hear gasped and turn in the direction of it.

My mom.

Tears fall down her face, just like the ones she shed when I left, and according to Emery, ones she spills all the time when I'm brought up. She's still as beautiful as she was four years ago. Long blonde hair that falls past her shoulders and eyes that twinkle in the light.

She starts a full-out run, and I halt, bracing myself for the impact I know is coming.

She collides with me, wrapping her arms around my neck. With her being a bit shorter than me, she must've leapt to get that leverage.

Sucking in deep, my mother shaking in my arms, the smell of sunshine fills me. She sobs as I hold her tight, feeling all the weight she's carrying around. My eyes don't close, though, because my father stands only feet away, arms crossed, glaring eyes trained on me.

"Austyn Kristina!" Aunt Princess screams as she marches up to us. She hasn't changed a single bit. Still full of fire as her attention directs on her daughter. "Who did this to you?" she barks, holding Austyn by the arms and inspecting her face.

My mom releases me and looks up, wetness staining her face. "You're really here." Her words are like a faint prayer, one that I'm sorry to break very soon.

"Hi, Mom."

She smiles hugely. "You're home!" She pulls me against her again, squeezing me tight, as if she were to let go of me, I'd disappear.

Princess' eyes cut to me, still blazing. "You know who did this to her?"

Well, hello to you, too. "Nope."

Princess is still the same. Black hair with red

throughout it, and still tough as nails. She doesn't look like she's aged a day.

Hell, the place in general hasn't changed. It still looks like it did when I left.

"You didn't think to find the bastard?" Her accusatory tone has my hackles rising. Fuck her if she thinks she's going to talk to me that way.

"Nope." It's a lie, of course. It ran through my mind several times on the drive here. When I get back to Grayson, I'll do something about it.

"Fucker. Can't depend on you for shit," she barks out, landing a direct blow.

I say nothing. There's no point. They have their opinions of me, so let them be. I gave up fighting to change anyone's view of me the day I made the decision to leave here. After all, if my father couldn't see me beyond my addiction and mistakes, no one would. Seems it's held true, even after all these years.

"Austyn, you good?"

Her eyes flash to me, and she shakes her head. "Don't go."

My mother releases me again and steps back. This surprises me, but as my father approaches, I can tell why.

The vein on his neck is ticking. He doesn't want me here anymore than I want to be here.

Men and women start filing out of clubhouse.

Guess they all want to see the fuckup that is Deacon Alexander Gavelson. Too bad they'll be disappointed.

"Well, look who the cat puked up," Nox says, coming up to the group.

I stare him down, waiting for whatever he throws at me next. I've learned a lot in the past four years. So much so, it would surprise everyone around here.

"Nox," Austyn chastises.

"I don't want to hear shit from you, Austyn. He the one who beat the shit out of you?"

This suggestion pisses me off to a point I feel my temper about to slip. Refusing to let it, I suck in a deep breath. This right here ... This is what my *family* thinks of me? That I beat the shit out of women. My younger woman cousin. Yep. That's me, fucker.

"Nox!" Austyn shouts, getting up in his face. "He'd never hit me, you moron!"

"Yeah right," Nox scoffs, looking back at me and snarling, "Fucker can't wait to get his hands on one of us."

"Shut the fuck up! You really are an asshole!" Austyn shouts.

Nox stalks over to me, our heights rivaling. Our body types are similar, too, but he doesn't have the years of fighting in the ring that I have.

"Fuck you," he says.

Again, I say nothing. I didn't come here to start a fight. However, that doesn't mean I won't end it.

Nox swings his fist out, ready to slam into my face, but I grip his fist hard, stopping it in mid-swing. Using my power, I squeeze, crushing his fingers together as I step into his space.

"You raise a hand to me again, you'd better be prepared. This isn't child's play anymore, Nox."

His face twists as he pulls out of my grasp. "Why don't you just do what you do best and get the fuck out of here." He steps back, the first smart move he's played.

"Deke, we need to talk." Surprisingly, this comes from my father.

I cross my arms over my chest. "Talk."

"My office." This one comes from the left. My uncle Cruz stands there with Cooper at his side. Both give me disapproving looks. What else is new in that department?

"Why? There's nothing to say," I respond, taking a glance around the space, my focus landing on a beautiful blonde with bluish-purple tips in her hair and her hands tucked into the back pockets of her jeans. She's toned in a way that tells me she works out, but it's something about those green eyes that I can see from here that stop me for a moment. They suck me in, and it takes strength to pull away from them.

Look at me. Here ten fucking minutes, and I'm already salivating over a club momma. Dumbass.

"Look, let's get real; none of you want me here

anymore than I want to be here. I did a solid for Austyn. She's home, safe and sound. No need for a talk that will prolong my leaving, which makes everyone here, including me, happy."

"Austyn, are you okay?" Ryker, one of the brothers, darts to Austyn's side, taking in her face. His features go hard. Then he moves to touch her face, and she jerks away. She then proceeds to take a couple of steps back from him.

Motherfucker. He's the father.

A red haze fills my vision as I stalk over to him, putting myself between him and Austyn. She's had a thing for him since as long as I can remember, and that fucker knocked her up.

I tightly grip his shirt and leather.

"You," comes out in a forceful growl.

Austyn moves quickly, inserting herself between us, her pleading eyes coming to me. "No, Deke," she says. "I swear it's not."

"Not what?" Ryker asks, throwing his arm out, but before it can connect, I push him back.

"Better not fuckin' be," I warn her as she continues to stand between us.

Her eyes beg me, pleading with me to drop it.

I search for the truth. If Ryker is the father, I'll beat his ass right here, right now, and dare one motherfucker in here to stop me.

The tender touch of her hand to my arm stops me. "Swear, Deke. Please stop."

"What the fuck's your problem?" Ryker moves in close, anger radiating from him. Good. Maybe he needs some sense knocked into his ass.

"You."

"Fuck off!"

"Ryker, enough," Cruz calls out, giving his order. That's exactly what it is.

Ryker reluctantly backs up a step, his eyes not leaving Austyn's.

"Care to tell me what the fuck that's about?" Ryker accuses Austyn.

"No, she fuckin' doesn't," I answer for her, and his response is a growl. "And stop askin' her questions like you give a shit. Go off with your momma."

"You sonofabitch!"

"Enough!" Cruz's voice rises to growling and authoritative. He's always had it, but now it seems to have a deeper edge to it. Guess that's what happens when you take over as president of a club. I wouldn't know. "Deke, my office. Now."

"I'm not really keen on orders, Cruz."

"Boy, now," my father says, coming closer.

I know what's going to happen. He's going to try to force me to do what he wants. Then I'll fight back and get the entire club in an uproar. If I just go in and see what the fuck these people have to say, then I can get the hell out of here.

"Fine, but only a few. I need to get back on the road."

"No," my mother says. "Come home for dinner, or we can go out—something. Just don't—"

"Mom, I'm leaving as soon as this is over."

Tears fall from her eyes.

"Swear to Christ, you make your mother cry one more damn time, I'm takin' it out of your hide."

"Really, ol' man? Good luck with that."

"Now, both of you," Cruz interrupts.

As I walk to the clubhouse, my eyes connect again with the blonde. I feel as if she's assessing me, trying to figure me out. Good fucking luck with that one, sweetheart.

CHAPTER EIGHT
Rylie

"I'M SORRY, BUT WE GOT FAMILY SHIT GOIN' DOWN," Princess says, walking up with a pretty young woman around my age, maybe a bit younger.

The girl has a busted lip, and her eye is a bit swollen, but I also notice her knuckles are red and swollen. Whatever happened to her, she fought back. Good. And from the fire breathing in her eyes, she's not one to back down easily. Tough woman. I like it.

"Understand. When do you want me to start?"

"Wait. What's going on?" the young woman asks, looking between the two of us, curiosity brimming.

"This is Rylie. She's taking over security at X. Get used to seeing her." Princess looks at me. "Rylie, this is my daughter Austyn." Ah, so this is the infamous Austyn. Word has it Princess taught all her kids how to fight, how to defend themselves.

Seems like she did a bang-up job with her daughter.

"Hi. You alright?"

Austyn's back straightens. "Of course. My mom taught all her kids well."

"I bet she did. When?" I prompt Princess, ready to get the hell out of there.

Something big is going down. The damn tension in the air is so thick and weighted it's liable to suffocate everyone if they stick around. It all centers around the gorgeous man who pulled up with Austyn. Deke, they called him.

He didn't look happy one bit to be here, so I guess there's bad blood somewhere. It was strange, though, for that split-moment when our eyes connected. A pulse ran through me, like he was pulling me to him. It was unnerving. I don't need that shit in my life. It must be hormones, and it's been a damn long time.

One asshole ex is enough for right now.

"Let me call you. I don't know how this is going to go." Princess gazes at her daughter who meets her intense eyes full-on, even lifting her chin.

Gotta say, I'm impressed. Most people would crumble under that kind of stare, but not her. It's all interesting. Very interesting.

"Sounds good."

"Mom, tell them to leave Deke alone. Seriously. He did me a favor, and now they're going to treat him like an enemy. He's not," Austyn starts as I try to make my exit from the scene.

I'm blocked by a damn table, which I don't like. Two options: one, hop over it, or two, tough it out.

"Why does he have all the cuts on his face, Austyn?"

"He's a fighter, Mom. You know this. It's not new. He didn't know I was coming and just got done with a fight. That's why his face is busted."

"And why the fuck is my daughter's face busted up? That was a stupid ass move." Princess gets in Austyn's face, but the girl still doesn't back down.

"I wanted to get away. I got jumped, took care of it, and went to Deke's. End of story."

I can't help watching Austyn's eyes. They're strong and determined. In the far recesses, though, something is wrong. For Austyn's sake, her mother better not pick up on that small tell. She'll nail her ass to the wall.

"Don't bullshit the bullshitter, Austyn." She sees it. Sucks for Austyn.

"Mom, just don't, alright!" Austyn explodes. "I'm not talking about it. I left. I'm back. I'm twenty-years-old, and just because I didn't tell everyone where I was going does not mean you all get to treat me like I'm a child! You didn't raise me to be stupid. Remember that."

As they stare each other down, I take that as my cue.

"Alrighty, I'm just going to get out of here and let you handle your business."

Princess steps to the side, allowing me to get through, not taking her focus off her daughter. That chick is going to have a rough night.

I glance a second longer than I should have at the door Deke went through, then shake my head. According to him, he's leaving. This is a good thing.

"Harder!" Charlie yells as he moves his body to the left then the right.

I nail him a couple of times, and all he does is chuckle. Fucker.

We go at it for another thirty minutes, all while thoughts of my time at the clubhouse run through my head. If nothing else, it should be an interesting job, if they can keep all their personal shit to themselves. Not that I need interesting, but it should change up the monotony a bit.

Really, if you think about it, a strip club isn't any different than a fight club. Both have guys high on testosterone and sexy women around.

My mind keeps going back to the tall, built man with anger all over him. Hell, even from far away, I could feel those waves bouncing off me.

Austyn said he was a fighter. In my experience, a lot of men fight to cut through the tension in their lives. True, they do it for money, too. But there always tends to be an underlying thing. I wish the curiosity of it would go away, but unfortunately, it's burning inside of me.

"Rylie, either get your head in the game or step the hell out!" Charlie calls out, snapping me out of my thoughts.

I halt mid-swing, coming back into the present. Damn. He's right. Motherfucker. When was the last time I got lost in myself? When I lost focus at the task I was doing? Shit, the last time I remember was when Aunt CB was on my ass while I was living with her. And that was a damn long time ago.

I need to get this man out of my head. Way out of my head. This shit is bad news all the way around. I don't lose focus. Ever. That's the moment you'll get killed. I'm not quite ready to go out yet. I fear, with that man, though, I'd go out in a blaze of glory.

Dumbass, you're not going to see him again. Ever.

"Sorry. I got this."

"What's goin' on, girl? This isn't you." He stares at me with those eyes that have looked to the heart of me for years. If I were to have a father, I'd want it to be Charlie. Except when he calls me on my shit. Or maybe it's especially because he calls me out on it. That's a toss-up.

"Startin' a new job, and it's on my mind."

Charlie puts his hands down and stares at me like I've grown horns and am spewing green slime from my mouth. "New job?"

I stretch my neck from side to side, stretching out the muscles. "I'm workin' over at X for a while as security."

"How the fuck did you get that job?"

Needing water, I lead us over to the bench and proceed to explain my run-in with Princess and how it ended with me and a job. He says nothing, which isn't like Charlie. He's an in-your-face kind of man, always wanting the best for everyone. Heart of gold, I tell ya.

He's also a meddler when it comes to me. Truthfully, I wouldn't have it any other way. At least he gives a shit, and that's more than I can say about the actual *family* I have.

"Give me somethin'," I finally say, gulping down a bottle of water. The coolness helps quench my thirst. Love working out, but damn am I always so thirsty.

"That club's been around for years. Know Pops. He was president for years. Handed over the reins to his boys, Cruz and GT." He shakes his head. "For a while, they were havin' some serious problems. Men comin' after their women. Of course, this is all hearsay. Not one of them would confirm or deny anything. But shit gets out. They've been pretty tame over there at that clubhouse. I just don't know if you going to work for them is a good idea."

"Why? I mean, I'm already in with Schade as it is."

"Yeah, I know. Just don't want you in any deeper than you are. Know you can hack it. Just want good for you."

My heart warms. He's always seen more to me than I ever have. He needs to give that up, though I'm really not ready for him to.

Hope is a powerful thing. Me, I love my life. If I didn't, I'd change it. But it's nice that he cares.

"This is my life, Charlie, and I'm good at it. Plus, Princess is paying me double what I make with Schade and is working around my schedule there."

His face softens. "Damn, she really wants ya."

"It appears so. That being said"—I rise from my seat—"need to practice, old man, or do you need a potty break?" I chide, seeing him smirk.

"Get your smartass out there. Let's do this."

Mind in the game, we work out.

CHAPTER NINE
Deke

HERE WE GO.

We walk down the hall, with Cruz in front of me, and my father, Cooper, and Nox behind me. I'm not sure yet if this is a family meet and greet, or club shit. Either way, it just needs to get over and done with so I can put miles between us.

All this pomp and circumstance. If they want to beat the hell out of me, I won't go down without a fight. But look how many there are. Along with the shit-ton of them that stared at us the entire way in here. They could take me out. That's a risk I took bringing Austyn here. I knew it, but I'm not sure it really sank in for her. Hell, maybe she doesn't give a shit. That's fine, too. Not saying I would have if she hadn't shown up on my doorstep.

Entering the room that was once Pops' office and now is obviously Cruz's feels strange. Like I don't belong. It's a feeling I know all too well.

"Sit," Cruz barks as I stand behind the chair.

I'm not one of his men he can order around. At one point in my life, that's all I wanted—to be part of this club, fit in, be a brother. Then that all blew up in my face.

Cruz shakes his head and plops in the chair, leaning back in it casually. When my dad and Nox take a seat, I do, too. No need to make this worse than it already is. I already proved my point.

"Good to have you home," Cruz starts, and my brow quirks. Good to have me home? These fuckers wanted me so far gone before, and they got their wish. Now he's happy I'm here? Right ...

"See you don't talk much, boy," my father says, elbows resting on his knees and head down, staring at the floor. "You clean?"

I'd have much preferred a punch to the temple than for my father to ask that question. I've been fucking clean since I left Sumner. Was I fucked up? Hell yeah. But the second stint in rehab did me in. The fact my father can't look at me and know I'm not high as a damn kite just proves he didn't know me then, and he sure as hell doesn't know me now.

Our relationship took hit after hit as the years went on. Sad, but it hasn't changed and never will.

Instead of answering my father, I look at Cruz. "She showed up at my place with her face a mess. I let her crash for the night and brought her here. She didn't tell me shit. Now, I need to go."

Cruz looks up at the ceiling, then slowly looks back down, eyes blazing at me. This is the man I remember. The ruthless, take no prisoners uncle who did the dirty work for Ravage. Looking up to him growing up was a mistake. It did nothing but make me want my place here more. It was all an illusion, this world and me.

"Answer the question," my father says from next to me while Cooper just eyes me, no doubt trying to read my expression. Good luck with that one, buddy. I learned a long time ago how to mask all that shit.

I don't owe these people a damn thing. I don't owe anyone anything. It pisses me off that I feel the damn need to answer. What the fuck is wrong with me? I need to just get up and walk the fuck out of here. And not look back.

"She's upset, so go easy on her," I say instead of answering again, turning to Coop. There's so much I need to say to him. I fucked up royally with him, not that it matters. I can admit when I'm a dick, though. "Sorry about the shit I said when I was a kid. Not gonna make excuses. It was shit, and I own it."

Staring at him, I wait for some sort of signal that he heard what I said, but he gives me nothing, so I move on.

"Alright, I'm out of here." I move to stand up, and my father rises with me, standing toe to toe with me.

"You're just going to leave again and let me pick up all the pieces that is my wife off the ground? Your mother, Deke! She fuckin' cries all the time ... still! Do you not give a shit about that?"

"There's nothing for me here. My life is in Grayson. You go on with your life. I go on with mine. She'll get over it, just like she did before."

He steps closer, anger pouring off him. Something else is working behind his eyes. If I had to guess, it'd be hurt, but that couldn't be.

"You fuckin' little shit. Get over it? She hasn't gotten over it for a single fuckin' day. Holidays are the worst. We don't even like celebrating them because she turns into a pile of fucking tears. And I can't stop them. Why? Because it's all you. You're not around, Deke."

He thinks I want this? That I want to hurt my mother? He doesn't have the least bit of a clue. I'm not sure if that or his words piss me off more.

"Then man up and fix your wife, Dad," I bark back as he throws his fist at me. I block and hold his hand firmly in mine. "Don't." I release him and push him back. Getting in a fight here is the least of my concerns.

My truck is calling for me to get the fuck out.

"You're worthless!" he yells, giving a direct hit. But, like the others, nothing makes me fall.

"Good to see your opinion of me hasn't changed."

"Stop bein' a dick," Cooper says from the chair across from his father. "It's time you come home."

Oh, so Cooper suddenly wants me around? When he turned eighteen, he couldn't be seen with me since I was younger. What the fuck ever! Always in his shadow and then tossed aside like yesterday's newspaper. *No thank you, Cooper Cruz. I am fine in life where I am.*

Inside, I laugh. My family. Yeah. No, wait. Emery isn't here; she's the only one I consider family. Maybe my mother a bit. Okay, and Austyn. Fuck ...

"I'm not comin' back here. None of you think any different of me than when I left. I'm not livin' like that." Every damn one of them turned their backs on me.

"You're missin' out on all the shit you need to be a part of," Coop continues. "Let the past go."

"Bud, I already let it go a long damn time ago. I'm leavin'." I turn to the door, reach for the handle, and turn it.

"Your mom's sick," my father says, making me still.

I turn around to find all eyes on my father. Some are in shocked horror. They're damn good actors.

"Bullshit. Emery would've told me."

He smirks. "Good to see you at least talk to her."

"Don't act like you don't know."

"Emery doesn't know. Angel didn't want to tell anyone until her appointment next week."

Cruz rises from his seat as Cooper and Nox get

closer. "Brother, don't you think you should have told me?" Cruz accuses.

Either my father is pulling a scam on all of us to get me to stay, or he's telling the truth. I hope to Christ he's lying.

"It's new, alright. Like I said, she didn't want anyone to know. She hasn't even told Princess."

"Fuck. What is it?" Cooper asks.

My father falls into the chair, threading his fingers through his hair then pulling hard. The tension is there, but it's not directed at me this time.

"Found a lump. Doctor had her do a mammogram. Tests didn't come back good. Now, she's doing chemo trying to get the shit out of her body. We're all hoping for the best here."

He's not shitting me. It's the truth.

The anger begins to bubble. I'm not sure if it's at the situation, or if I'm pissed at myself. Nevertheless, it hits in a heated rush.

My fists clench, and my body gets tight. The urge to hit something comes hard and fast. I turn toward the paneled walls and crash my fist through the wood. Pulling out, I see the blood drip. I don't give a fuck if I bleed. This is so fucked up. Between my mother and Austyn ... fucking hell.

A hand comes to my shoulder, and I turn in a rush, fist up to make contact. Any reason to fight, just give it to me.

Cooper holds his hands up. "Calm your shit. We got kids out there who don't need to hear this."

My body heaves for air as the carefully constructed walls of my life begin to bend. No, that can't happen. No bending. No swaying. None of that.

Air. I need it.

Darting to the door, I get the fuck out of there, my father, uncle, and cousins yelling my name. Down the hall and into the clubhouse, the need to hit something grows. I need to get this anger out, and I need to do it now.

"Deke?" I hear my mother's voice.

I can barely shove down the lump in my throat. Trying to ease a bit, I take her in my arms and kiss her cheek. "I need to get out of here for a bit, but I'll be back."

"Promise?" she asks, pulling back and looking into my eyes.

"Promise. But you gotta let me go right now, okay?"

Tears fall from her eyes. "Okay," she whispers as my father rounds the corner.

"Deacon Alexander!" he roars.

I pay him no mind. I kiss my mother on top of her head then exit the building, not stopping to talk to anyone. Not bothering to even blink.

I hop in the truck, peel out as quickly as I can, and drive. That's all I can do—drive.

Even after an hour on the road, the anger still

burns inside of me. Nothing like the stench of death to put things in perspective. Fuck, but I don't want to be here. However, it's not looking like I have a damn choice. Motherfucker.

I need to punch something hard and for a long time. The tension inside me needs to come out. I know exactly who to go to.

Steering the truck that way, thoughts run rampant of my mother being sick. Sick?

An ache grows in my cold chest, feeling like a thousand knives stabbing me at the same time. She's a good woman. Always has been. She did a great job raising Emery and me. Too bad I had to go fuck shit up.

The notion that she'll have to do radiation, chemo, or lose parts of her body is the coldest fucking douse of water I've ever felt in my life. Yet, I hate it here. Okay, maybe not here, but I do hate the thoughts of being here in this town. Hell, the way I was flat-out accused of hitting Austyn was a punch to the gut. Like I'd ever hit her. It pisses me off they think so little of me. Then, to ask if I'm still using. They have no fucking clue. Not one clue. Staying here will be a problem. I just know it. Not just family shit, either.

The anger builds as I turn into the gym I came to four years ago when I needed to get away from my family and let the rage that burned inside escape.

Parking and hopping out of the truck, I make my

way to the door and swing it open. The sounds of grunts and strains echo throughout the space as I move to the front desk where a tiny little girl, who can't be more than eighteen, sits. Her eyes gleam as I step forward. Considering the anger coming off me, this is surprising. Most would want to get as far away from me as possible.

"Can I help you?" She rises as she asks the question, her tight as hell bra stretched thin over her tits. So much so her nipples point directly at me. Not to mention the flat abdomen that leads to shorts that I'm pretty positive are underwear. No matter where I go, this is the shit that comes along—women eager enough to fuck me here on the desk if I'd let them.

"Charlie here?"

"Yeah, he's training someone. Let me get him." She gives me a wink as she strides around the desk, making sure to sway her hips a bit more than she needs to. She's super thin, which is fine, but a big man like me likes to have something to grab on to. She'd do for an after-fight fuck, but nothing else.

I follow her as she moves, seeing Charlie sparring with a very attractive female. Blonde hair pulled back into a knot on top of her head, and I swear I see some blue in there. Her back is to me, and what a fine ass she has. Round and full, giving my hands something to grip.

Charlie holds up his arms as the woman strikes

each of them, going back and forth. They both have sweat glistening their bodies, but damn hers is sexy as all hell.

She turns, still swinging away, and it takes me a moment, but ... that's the woman from the clubhouse. What the hell is a club momma doing here fighting? A woman like her could hold her own to just about anyone. Most of the time, the mommas in the clubhouse are there for protection of some sort. This woman doesn't need that.

The woman from the counter calls into the ring. Charlie holds up both of his hands, and the bombshell stops. There's conversation I can't hear going on. Then, when the petite woman points in my direction and Charlie sees me, a wide smile comes across his face.

Bombshell woman's eyes grow round at seeing me, so she must have been paying attention at the clubhouse.

Charlie holds up one finger and starts to come my way, taking the paddles off his hands as he moves. The old man still looks the same as when I came here regularly. He used to tell me that he let me come free because it was better than me going out and fighting on the streets.

"Deke?" he asks with a wide smile on his face, holding his hand out to me, which I take.

"Charlie, good to see ya."

"Shit, boy. What, four years?"

"Lookin' like that. I need to let off some steam. Can I use one of your bags."

His eyes turn curious. He knows about me, my family, the Ravage MC. Hell, it wouldn't surprise me if he knew about my time in Grayson, as well. The man knows his shit.

"Sure thing. You in town for long?"

"No clue yet. Just family shit."

"Damn, you've grown up, boy. Never thought I'd see the day that the scrawny kid would come in here a full-grown man."

"I wasn't scrawny, old man."

"And I'm not old," he fires back, then tilts his head to the bags. "Go on. We'll talk after."

I nod then make my way over to the bag. My gaze falls on the woman with blue hair again, and I lift my chin.

She shakes her head, a small smile playing on her plump lips. Fuck, those lips ...

I break away, go to the bag, strip my shirt, and begin to lay it all out. The anger, not being good enough, the never being what my father wanted—nothing else exists except for those thoughts and my fists connecting with the bag repeatedly.

Taping up would've been the smart thing to do, considering I feel the blood from my hands from last night's fight. It doesn't stop me from laying it all out there, though.

I feel the eyes on me, but block it all out and let the pain come through each of the strikes.

CHAPTER TEN
Rylie

ME, LIKE EVERYONE ELSE IN THE PLACE, CAN'T KEEP MY eyes off Deke as he lays into the bag. Each of his movements is calculated and precise. I've been around enough fighters to know that Deke's form is one of someone well-trained. His cut body also tells me that he works out regularly.

With each thrust into the bag, his back muscles contort and move. Not to mention the sexy as hell angel on his back. It's almost like she's dancing with each movement.

I can't deny the man is hot. He has a temper, obviously, but if my family would have accused me of hitting a relative, I'd be pissed, too. Yeah, I overheard that. Wish I hadn't.

This, though, the way he's striking the bag, moving his feet, his drawn down eyes, seems to be more.

Not your business.

"You gonna stare at him or finish?" Charlie asks.

"Can't help it. He's nice to look at."

Charlie finishes putting his paddles back on. "That boy has so much potential. Knew it when he left. Still know it now. Wish he'd live up to it."

"What do ya mean?"

He sighs. "Came here five or so years ago. Got into some trouble with drugs. Bad ones. His folks put him in rehab. First time didn't stick. The second time, he got out and left town. Left everyone behind."

"Don't ya think there was a reason?"

"Said he needed to get clean." He throws a thumb over his shoulder, indicating Deke. "He look like an addict to you?" I shake my head. "My guess is he cleaned up his shit when he left, but still don't know exactly why he took off, and definitely don't know why he's home now. Bet his momma's happy, though. She misses him like you wouldn't believe."

"You seem to know him well." Charlie's never mentioned him. Really, why would he? There was no reason in any of our time together to do so.

"Nah, there's more to that boy than anyone will ever crack. He's deeper than he leads on. More going on in that head. But he won't let it out. Punching shit gives him the out." He turns back to me. "You gonna put up or shut up?"

"Put up, old man."

"Ya know, I'm gettin' tired of you youngins sayin' that shit."

"Fits you. Ready?"

For the next twenty minutes, we finish my workout. I'm wringing wet with sweat. Luckily, my focus is on each throw and not the many grunts off in the distance.

I sit on the bench, chugging a water, towel around my neck that I just used to wipe off all the sweat pouring out of me. My breathing is starting to calm down, and my body feels damn good. Well used.

Charlie moved over to Deke after finishing with me. They have idle chitchat, but Deke doesn't look too much like a talker, and Charlie realizes it and moves off.

Syd, the receptionist, has drool running down her face. I really can't blame her. He's damn fine.

Enough staring. Time for me to get out of here.

I grab my bag and stuff my shit inside. The gym has a shower, but I'd rather use mine at home.

The bag is light. I fling it over my shoulder. One last look won't kill me.

When I do, our eyes connect, and a cool heat—if that's possible—slides over my skin like a caress. Damn, it's a beautiful feeling, and so new to me. *Get out.* Right.

Saying nothing, I march my ass toward the door, but in doing so, I have to pass by him. Why I even care is beyond me. Normally, guys can kiss my ass. Him, I could think of a lot of other things he could kiss.

Stop it and go get laid, woman!

"Hey." The deep voice comes from my left, and my feet instantly stop from the sound.

When I look up, I see sweat dripping down Deke's face, over his high cheekbones, and down to his sensuous lips. His hair is a light brownish-blond color, but wet, it looks much darker. All this makes me wonder what he'd look like right out of the shower.

"Hey."

He says nothing back, so I turn to move away. No sense in sticking around for a mundane conversation if he's not going to talk.

"Deke," he says, and I tilt my head toward him again. "You are?"

"Not sure you should know that."

A smirk plays on his lips, but it's devilish, kicking my curiosity in gear again. "Why's that?"

"Don't know you."

"You've seen me twice, and you know I have family in the club." He reads me well. I'm not sure if I like that or not. "Name isn't gonna kill ya."

"You never know about that."

He shrugs. "Alright." Deke begins to wipe the towel over his pecs, arms, and abs, then back to his face and hair. "Gotta split, anyway." He came in with nothing, but he puts the towel around his neck and begins to walk out.

"Rylie."

This gets his attention, and he stops. "Rylie, you a momma?"

My brows knit as I think about what he's talking about. *A momma?*

"No, I don't have any kids." That must be one of the most bizarre questions I've been asked in my life.

For some reason, he finds humor in this.

"Club momma."

"Not followin', big guy."

"Club whore, Rylie. Are you one of them?"

Shock hits first. Then I let it roll off. Of course. I didn't put those two together.

I can't help chuckling. "No, Deke, I'm not a club momma."

"Then why were you at the clubhouse? Someone's ol' lady?"

I cross my arms over my chest. "You sure have a lot of questions."

"I like to know the people around me." He tosses his towel over his shoulder.

"And you think I'm going to be around you?"

"Tryin' to figure that out."

Inwardly, I sigh. "I work at X."

"Ah, so you're a stripper." His gaze sweeps my body. "Can totally see that."

"You're a dick. No, I'm head of security, asshole."

"What?"

"Look, this Q and A session is lots of fun, but I have places to be." I start to move when he grabs my arm. The heat from him goes straight to my core. I hate that he does that to me. He's a dick. Just like every other man on the planet.

"Like I said, I need to know who I'm dealing with."

"Now you know. Have a nice life." I look down at his hand still holding me, searing me with his heat. "You can let go of me now."

"Not sure I can do that."

My breath hitches. Is this a wanting-to-kick-my-ass comment, or a you're-hot-let's-fuck one?

"Why's that?'

"No fuckin' clue."

"You're obviously goin' through some shit from what I saw at the clubhouse—deal with that." This, of course, is the smart thing to say, but my body is seriously protesting.

"Come for a drive with me."

"Big guy, I don't know you. What makes you think I'm going to get into a car with you?"

"Truck."

"What?"

"You're getting into a truck."

"Whatever. You know what I mean."

He releases my arm and swipes his shirt off a chair

then slips it on. "I'm not gonna force ya. You don't want to, don't."

"Where are we going?"

"Just drivin'. You can catch me up on all things Sumner."

"Why? You stayin'?"

His face turns a bit pained, and I regret asking the question, but he answers. "Lookin' like I'll be here more than I want to. Not a big deal, Ry. I'm out. See ya around."

My gut tells me it is a big deal. One of those situations that happens when you don't know the outcome, but whatever it is, it could be enormous in life. Like something hangs in the balance here, like a dangling carrot. My damn curiosity is kicking my ass, wondering what this is about. Not to mention he called me Ry. No one has done that since my parents.

"Fine, but if I tell you to stop, you stop."

"As long as you know I'll kiss you when we stop."

My lungs seize, and breaths become hard to intake. What in the Sam hell is wrong with me? Getting flustered over a man isn't my thing. Why him?

"Move before I change my mind." Which I totally should do, like, right this minute.

As we get to his monstrosity of a truck, he opens the door for me. I can't remember the last time ... Oh, yeah, I can. It was when my parents were alive. My father would always open the door for my mother, and then do the same for me. I always waited for him to finish so he'd do mine next. I felt like a princess in a castle every single time.

Damn, I miss him. I miss them. I miss a time when life seemed simple. Everything gets complicated the older you get.

I study the man who has captured my intrigue. Nothing about Deke is remotely simple.

Deke rounds the truck, hopping in and cranking the engine. Thank goodness my deodorant is holding up after that workout. I should've gone home and taken a shower.

After a while, driving in silence is driving me nuts. Idle time isn't something I allow myself. If I'm not at work, then I want to be working out, going out, not remaining still.

"So, what are we doing, exactly?" I pause. "Besides driving."

"The bag helped clear my head a bit, and I don't have my bike here, so I'm driving to clear the rest of it out."

"You want to talk about it?"

"Babe, do I look like the talkin' about my feelings type?"

No, no, he didn't, but there had to be a reason that I was sitting in his truck with him driving all over the place.

"Why security?" he asks after a beat.

"It's what I do."

"Why is it what you do?"

I think for a moment, never being asked this direct question before, recalling the reason I started in the first place. It's not a happy memory, but it's the reality of life. It's also something that I don't share with people, or at least, never felt compelled to tell anyone.

"What about you? You're a fighter?" I ask instead of answering.

"Ry, need you to talk to me. Tell me about you and clear my mind of some shit."

The man seems like a broody type who doesn't talk much, and for some reason, he's not acting that way with me. Hell, even with his family earlier, he didn't say much. It makes me curious to know more. Damn, don't they say curiosity killed the cat? Hopefully I don't end up dead.

I look out at the open road before us, watching the yellow dashes go by in a rush. Thoughts of my past invade me, one after another, and before I know it, I'm speaking.

"Grew up on the streets. You don't get by without learning to defend yourself. It wasn't a career path or anything like that. It just turned out that my defensive moves were pretty good and got better with each day that passed. I started as a bouncer at a couple clubs, but they were boring. Then I moved up. Now I do what I do."

"How old were you?"

"When I lived on the streets?"

"Yeah."

"Eighteen. Really sixteen because, technically, I had a home. I just wasn't welcomed in it." Aunt CB made that a reality at every turn she could, and still does.

"Why?"

"Are you one of those wiz people who's gonna turn everything I say against me somehow?"

A slow smirk tips his lip. It's sexy as all hell. "Nah. Just curious."

"Right." I turn back to the window. "When I was sixteen, my parents were killed, and I went to live with my aunt. She's a bitch and made sure to let me know how big of one she was every time she saw me. I was never good enough. I didn't do things the way my mother did. I looked like my mother. I ate my apple just like my mother. Hell, anything I did, she compared me to her sister. Not to mention the fact she wishes it were me lying six feet under and not my mother. Can't say I blame her there."

"Don't say that shit." His words come out with a bite that makes bumps rise on my arms. Not much makes me feel this way. I'm surprised he does.

Ignoring it and moving on, I say, "It was easier to live on the streets and not deal with her bullshit all the time."

"Not good enough, huh?"

It takes me a bit aback that that's the one thing he really got out of it, but I answer, "Never."

His grip on the steering wheel gets tighter, but his focus stays on the road. I wish I could get in that head of his.

CHAPTER ELEVEN
Deke

FUCK ME. THE CONNECTION I FELT WHEN I LAID EYES ON her at the clubhouse is proving deeper than surface. This is more than attraction. This is a pull stronger than any drug I've had pump through my veins.

Of all the things to connect us, it must be our sense of unworthiness from our families. I hate that shit for her, because I've lived it all my life. I know how it eats at your insides, festers and turns to anger.

The thing is, she doesn't seem angry. No, instead, she comes across as strong, independent, and happy. The way she speaks, she has a damn good head on her shoulders.

"You said your parents were killed."

I hear her breath heave, no doubt from a topic she doesn't want to talk about.

I know I'm pushing her, but I need the distraction.

The gym didn't ease the tension, frustration, and so many years of anguish. I need to focus on something other than myself.

"Yeah. Drive-by shooting. They were in their home, shots rang throughout the house, and within moments, I became parentless."

"Damn, babe. Sorry."

When I was younger, I wanted to be my father more than anything. I wanted to be by his side. I wanted to have my bike next to his, the Ravage MC cut on my back, and all the brothers at my back. It was all I ever wanted. All I desired, even at a young age.

Around me was family all the time. Cooper and I raised hell. Then shit went bad with him and Nox, and I raised hell. I always had someone at my back, doing stupid shit and getting in trouble more times than I can count.

All it took for me was a hit, one. One bad decision turned into years of fucked up shit. One hit easily turned into two. Then three ... Then I couldn't stop. The escape away from life was too much to not grab ahold of and embrace. There was no thinking. No control. No nothing, but me on the high of my life. It wasn't about Ravage, Cooper, shit I lost, shit I wanted and would never have. It was easy.

Then that high wasn't enough, and so on, until my folks threw me in rehab. I needed it before the crud I was hitting killed me, but it is still a craving inside me that's more intense than anything I've ever had.

"Shit happens in life. You play the hand you're dealt."

"Right," I agree, staring out at the road before me, my mother flashing through my head.

Cancer. The thought is a punch to the gut.

When I think back, really think back, my mother always defended me. I always wondered if she really accepted me for me. If she actually thought I was a total fuck up in my life or somehow could see through the bullshit. It's been so long I shouldn't care, but fuck, I do. She's my mom.

Listening to Rylie and the fact she lost her mother and father, I realize I'm not ready for that shit. Not to mention a fuck of a lot of time I've wasted.

Fuck, there are consequences, though, if I stay. Somehow, I need to figure that shit out, too.

I rub my hand over my face and through my hair.

"If you want to talk about it, it's lookin' like I'm not goin' anywhere."

The last time I let someone carry the weight of my shit was back when Coop and I were tight. He took my shit, helped me sort it, and then we moved on. Even young, he knew how to solve pretty much everything. That's what I admired most about him.

Since him, there's been no one. Not Nox. Not the dozens of therapists in rehab. Not the support groups.

Not the specialists. Not the doctors. No one. It's all been on me. I can take it. I've done it for four years now. The thought of dumping it on someone else and letting them carry the load is tempting.

But it's not happening.

I gave into temptation too many times. I won't do it again, no matter what.

We drive for a while in silence that isn't uncomfortable. It's peaceful in a way I don't get, yet I take it. I need it. I need peace.

Pulling off into a cove I remember from back in the day, I throw the truck in park, knowing I shouldn't do what I'm about to do. With all the shit swirling around me, I need to keep focus. Right now, though, I crave distraction.

Fuck it.

Pushing my seat all the way back, I reach over and unlatch Rylie's belt.

"What are you doing?" she asks.

I grab her hand and pull her onto my lap so she's straddling me. She brings her hands to my chest hard, putting pressure on me, pulling away.

Rylie's breath catches, shock written on her face. She begins to speak, but I pull her down to my lips and take. She resists a bit, pressing on my chest, but I hold steady. Seconds later, she's not resisting anymore. Quickly, I'm not taking anymore. No, she's giving, and damn does she give. She clenches my shirt as the truck heats up quickly.

I learn two things very fast. One, Rylie is a hellcat. She takes what I give her and gives it back hard. Two, she's hot for me. Burning so much her hips are grinding hard on my cock.

Squeezing her tit, she groans in my mouth. She tastes of cinnamon and sweetness.

Then she breaks away, heaving, her eyes looking deeply into mine, penetrating.

"You sure you want this, cowboy?" she teases, her body telling me she's all in.

"Fuck yeah."

"This means nothing. Just two people fucking. Got me?" she demands.

Considering I don't want to be in this town, I'm game for that.

"Got it."

She climbs off, taking off those fucking tight-ass shorts and her underwear, and pulling off her shoes. She comes back, her eyebrow quirked. "You havin' second thoughts, big man?"

"Fuck no." I pull her down and kiss her again as she roams her hands over my body, each touch searing me and going straight to my hard cock.

She unbuttons my jeans. With swift maneuvers, I unleash my dick, wrap it, and slide inside of her. Her groan of pleasure is nowhere near enough.

"Wanna hear you scream."

"Make me," she challenges.

Gripping her hips, I shove in and out of her, her head hitting the ceiling of the truck. She groans, gripping my shoulders. Somehow, she finds leverage with her legs and uses them to slam down as I push up.

The feel, the friction, her tight cunt wrapped around my cock, I lose it. She loses it. Rylie comes hard and loud, screaming my name, then burying her head in my neck. Gripping her tight, I find my release. Our breathing ragged, my cock still twitches.

After long moments, Rylie's body begins shaking. My first thought is she's crying. I don't have a fucking clue what that's from. Then I hear it. Laughter.

She's laughing.

"Babe, never had a woman laugh after I fucked her before."

She lifts herself up, a smile on her face. "Not bruisin' your ego, big man. Just didn't have this planned for the day."

"Plans fuckin' blow, Ry. And just sayin', my cock still inside of you." I press up, and her eyes become hooded. "Babe, it ain't no laughin' matter."

"Are you ready to go again?" she asks as I harden.

"Fuck yeah."

"Already?"

I set about showing her exactly how I can handle round two.

PULLING BACK INTO THE GYM, a weird vibe comes through the cab of the truck. We didn't talk a whole lot, but it was comfortable. Not once did she clam up on me or get that quiet where women want more but aren't saying anything. Never got that from her. If anything, she was relaxed and sated.

I toss the truck into park, knowing I need to get back to the clubhouse and talk to my mother, but also knowing this'll be the last time I'll see Rylie. It's been a long fucking time since I thought about seeing a woman again, but I wouldn't mind seeing her.

"Babe."

Ry turns toward me, her face contorting as she bursts out laughing.

"Not sure what the fuck's funny."

"It's cool, Deke. I get you. Get where you're comin' from. You got shit. I got shit. We needed a breather, and we got it from each other. Not gonna start stalkin' your ass or anything."

My lips tip up. "That's good."

"Yeah." She turns and hops out of the truck. "You know where to find me." She gives me a wink then slams the truck door shut, striding off. Her tight ass sways as she goes, making my cock hard once again.

Fuck.

She swings up into a kickass Jeep then takes off, not looking back once.

"Deke!" Austyn runs up to my truck as I get out. Back at the clubhouse again. Back where everything started.

"Surprised they took your leash off."

"Ha, ha. Didn't know you had a sense of humor."

"I don't."

"Whatever." She crosses her arms. "They didn't think you were coming back. Your ma's havin' a hard time, and your dad's fuckin' furious. You sure you wanna go back in there?"

"Fuck no. Don't got a choice."

"What's goin' on?" she asks, her brow tipping over the top of her sunglasses.

"Mom's got cancer."

Her hands drop, and she takes a step back like I physically punched her in the gut. "What?" Guess my old man was right in the everyone doesn't know pool. Least I know it's not a ploy to keep me here, but fuck me, I wish it was.

"Gotta go in and talk to her. Don't know a lot about it yet, but I'm sure it'll get around quick."

"Fuck, Deke." She steps forward, placing her hand on my arm as a show of comfort. It feels foreign and surreal. Comfort isn't a luxury I've had, even if it was my own doing.

"Gonna crash at your place tonight before I head back."

Surprise lights up her face. "You're stayin'?"

"The night. Go from there."

"No problem. You can stay as long as you want."

"The night, Austyn."

She nods and falls into step with me as I move toward the clubhouse. Spotting my mother sitting at a table, with Princess, Tanner, and a couple of the ol' ladies around her, I move that way. My father steps into my path, his look pissed as hell.

"Surprised you came back."

"Told Mom I would."

"What the fuck is wrong with you?" He crosses his arms over his chest, the vein ticking in his neck and his eyes piercing me to the spot.

"Besides my mom bein' sick? Nothin'."

"I don't want shit around her, Deke. I swear to fuck, you bring that around your mom, I'll end you."

His words hit me deep, sending me back to a time when I wasn't what he needed me to be. What he thought I should be. How I disappointed him and everyone around me. Not only do they cut, they burn. So much so my heartrate picks up. Still, I keep my shit together.

When I was a boy, this man was all I aspired to be.

Loyal, trustworthy, treated my mom like fucking gold. Then, one day it all twisted. I can't remember the exact moment because it was a series of them. He'd be pissed if anyone judged him, but he judged me before I even had a chance. Coop was years older than me, so of course he had his shit together before me. But comparing me to him, my actions, letting everyone in the clubhouse know, that disappointment made me lose respect for him. I'm pretty sure it'll never come back.

Where was his loyalty to me? Where was the love for me? Where was the ride on for me? With my dad, it was non-existent, or maybe I just didn't see it clearly.

I meet his stare head-on, not flinching, not cowering, not taking his shit. "Haven't touched that shit in four fuckin' years, *Dad*. Don't believe me. I don't give a fuck. I'm here for her, not you."

He moves closer into my space. "Fuckin' talk to me like that again, I'll pound you into the ground."

"Try it."

His eyes flare.

My mother comes between us, pushing her body in the small space. "Stop it! Stop it right this minute!"

I step back, only to allow her room. Eyes are on us everywhere, and I feel the air in the room change.

"This is enough!" she yells, and it comes out as a cry. "I love you, but you need to stop right now, GT."

"Angel—"

"No!" she barks, catching my father's undivided attention. "Deke and I are going out to the courtyard. Don't come out. I want to talk to my son."

"I think *we* should talk to him," my father counters, obviously not ready to give up.

"No, *we* aren't. You won't keep yourself in check, GT, and I need to actually talk to Deke. No yelling, no jabs, no fighting—talk to him. Once you can figure out how to do that, then *we* will talk to him. Right now, *I'm* going to."

My father pushes. "I—"

"If you come out there, GT, you'll be sleepin' on the couch." Fire roars in my mother's eyes.

"No way in hell, woman."

She steps closer. "Try me." It comes out in a growl, and I gotta say, I'm proud of my mom. She's been a fighter my whole life. Even before that, if the stories are all correct. That's how I know she'll beat this shit. She won't let it get her down.

My mother grabs my hand and pulls me out of the clubhouse and into the grassy area. She goes to a picnic table off to the side with no one around.

"Sit," she orders, and I do as she says because she's on a roll and because I want answers as well as she does.

She sits in front of me, a slow smile coming to her beautiful face. Damn, I've missed that smile. Having it directed at me and feeling it is like a kick in the gut.

Sunshine. She smelled it, radiated it, is it, and I've missed years. Damn.

"I'm so damn happy you're here. Talk to me."

No way am I going to lie and tell her I'm happy to be here. I'd rather have my nails pulled out by the roots.

She reaches out, and I take her hands in mine. They're a bit cold to the touch, so I give them a thumb rub.

"They say I'm sick. Don't look it, don't feel it, but it's there. We're hopin' it hasn't spread, because that's the best-case scenario right now."

The words hit me like lead bullets.

"You know for sure it's cancer?"

"Yeah, Deke. That's what I'm getting treated for."

"Fuck."

Her hands tighten in mine. I'm thankful for that small bit of reassurance, even if I should be giving it to her. "The chemo isn't bad yet, but they say it'll get worse as time goes on."

"You'll beat it," I demand with all my power.

This time, her smile doesn't reach her eyes, showing me her fear. "Yeah. Tell me about you. What are you doing? Where are you working? Do you have a woman in your life?"

"I'm a mechanic. Make decent money."

She surprises me with, "You're fighting?"

"Yep." I'm not stupid in thinking that I haven't been

looked into. I may not have been around, but the Ravage MC doesn't leave things to chance.

Her brows draw together. "Why?"

"It's part of who I am now, Mom. I get paid damn good for what I do."

"Bet you do. Can't see you takin' scraps."

I smirk. "Never take scraps from anyone. That's what you've always said."

"Right. You deserve the best." She pauses, squeezes my hand, and then goes for it. "The drugs gone for good?"

For some reason, it doesn't irritate me coming from her as opposed to my father. "Yeah. Clean four years."

"But you left four years ago."

"Yep."

"Then why'd you go?" She asks the question I don't want to answer. Ever.

I blow out. "Just had to, Mom. Not talkin' about that shit."

She gives my hands a squeeze. "I want you home."

"I can visit."

"No, Deke. I want you home with your family. With me. I need you here," she pleads.

Fuck. There is so much to me coming here that she has no idea about.

"Don't know if I can do that, Ma. Got a life up north."

"You've got family down here," she counters.

Family, the word churns inside me like acid.

"You know damn well that none of those motherfuckers want me here. I was accused of hitting Austyn, for Christ's sake. That's how much they think of me. I'm not livin' like that."

"And I'm not going to fight for my damn life and not have my kids around. You've been gone four years too long, Deacon Alexander. You think they don't want you here? Prove you deserve it. Prove you're not who they think. Man up and pull your head out of your ass. I'm not having another family function without my *whole* family here. I'm not having holidays without my *entire* family here. No more missing pieces. You want me to fight? Then you fight with me."

I pull away from her and lean back on the bench, the weight of everything she just said laying heavy on my shoulders.

"Are you tellin' me you're not gonna fight this shit unless I'm here?" Talk about a sock to the gut.

She pierces me with her gaze, giving me the one she used to when she was angry with me or wanted me to listen. "I'm tellin' you, your ass is here. Go get your shit sorted and come home."

"That didn't answer my question."

"That's all you're gettin'."

I'm pretty fucking sure my mother just threw down on me. The absolute shit thing is, I have no retort. Sure, I can be a dick and refuse, go up to Grayson, and forget all this shit. But she's my mom. If anything happens to her, my sister would lose it ... my father would crumble.

I run my hand through my hair, gripping it tight. "Can't believe my mother is blackmailing me."

A small tip of her lips tells me she knows exactly what she's doing and doesn't give two shits about it.

"You're gonna beat this."

She leans forward, the determination I wanted moments ago making its appearance. "Yes, I am."

The decision is done. "Gotta go home and get shit sorted."

Surprise and wonder cloud her eyes as she pulls back from the table, waiting for the answer, yet preparing for a verbal blow when she asks, "This mean you're comin' home, right?"

"Gotta talk to my boss. Not sure how all that'll fly."

"Need you back here Saturday. Your sister's comin' home, and I want you here."

Inwardly, I groan, not wanting my sister to have to deal with this shit.

"You think this is gonna go smooth, you're mistaken."

"I don't care. You're home, that's all that matters."

Warmth fills me for the first time in years. "You always had my back."

She stands up from the table, and I follow. She

wraps me in her arms. "Always. I'll always have your back, never doubt that."

Damn, I missed my mom.

After talking to my mom, I call Austyn, telling her my ass is going home. Home. Guess it's not going to be home anymore.

CHAPTER TWELVE
Rylie

THE MUSIC THUMPS THROUGH THE SPEAKERS AND THE floor vibrates under my feet as I make my pass around the floor at X. My senses are alert, watching everyone and anyone, looking for things that don't belong or are out of the ordinary. Being on this side of the party is much different than in the chairs.

Three days so far at X. Each one had some sort of surprise, which is good for a woman like me. Nothing like Schade's, though. This is way calmer, and I'm not a hundred percent it's going to keep my interest. We shall see.

Princess crosses the floor throughout the night. The first night, she asked me repeatedly if everything was okay. It always was. The second night, she let up a bit. Tonight, she's only been by twice, to which I'm thankful.

Six days since I fucked a man I didn't know in a truck on the side of the road. Six days of my body throbbing. Six days of my mind playing weird tricks on me. Six days of thinking about him. Six days of me kicking my own ass for doing all the things above.

A woman catches my eye, stalking into the club. One, because she's stalking. Two, she looks furious. And three, her eyes just narrowed and she's huffing it to someone. She's a cute thing with a bob haircut that frames her round face perfectly. Except, right now, that face is contorted with pure rage.

I clock the guy her gaze is fixated on. Kara, one of the dancers, is giving him a very nice lap dance. Knowing this will end bad for everyone involved, I make my way over and intercept the woman whose gaze is burning a hole into the man.

"What do we have here?"

Her piercing eyes come to me. "What do you want?"

"Security, ma'am. Can I help you?"

"Janet!" the man practically yells, sending Kara flying off his lap when he stands up quickly and comes over.

"You piece of shit!" the woman yells at the man, just as she reaches out and slaps him hard across the face.

Wrapping my arm around her waist and pulling her back, I look at the man. "Out."

Me, I don't give a shit what their squabbles are. What I care about is getting these two the fuck out of there. After accomplishing this, I move back to my rounds.

Yeah, not sure if this is going to keep my attention.

The next few hours go by smoothly. I can't wait until closing time.

I toss my bag over my shoulder and move out the back door. My feet give a slight falter, but recover quickly when I see Deke standing beside my Jeep. What the hell?

"Deke," I greet, moving closer.

When I get within arm's reach, he tugs me behind my neck, pulls me to him, then crashes his lips down on mine. Holy mother of Mary, this man can kiss. His lips are soft, yet his kiss is hard, unyielding, and demanding.

I move my hands to his leather jacket and hold on to him, giving him back what he's giving me. Arousal spikes. I need friction. Damn, do I need it.

He breaks away and looks into my eyes. "Need to fuck you, but want a bed."

In a haze that is Deke, I stupidly say, "My place. Follow me."

He kisses me then sets me in my Jeep before shutting the door.

It's not until I'm practically home that I realize what I've just done. I invited him to my house, my safe haven. Shit. There goes the don't-bring-men-to-the-house rule, right out the damn window.

Pulling in, Deke has my door opened before I do, pulling me up and into his arms. Any other man manhandled me like this, I'd kick his balls into his teeth. He's lucky I like his cock.

He lifts me, and I wrap my legs around his waist, our lips going at each other like starving animals.

Somehow, he gets the keys from me and unlocks my door. Only then do I hear the beeping of the alarm and come up for breath as I slide my legs down.

"Give me a sec."

I do my thing, turning it off, just as I hear the paws tapping on the floor. Hope Deke likes dogs.

"Hey, bud," I hear as I enter the room. Brewer's paws are up on Deke's chest, and Deke's petting him. Brewer goes in for a lick, and Deke steps back. "No lickin'."

I swear I hear Brewer whine. *Get in line, buddy. I wanna lick him, too.*

"Deke, meet Brewer."

"He gonna watch while I fuck you?"

"Probably."

Deke charges forward, kissing me and sucking the life from me. "Don't give a fuck."

Damn those lips. All things Brewer are forgotten as Deke consumes me.

I jump up, wrapping my legs around his waist and

propping myself up with my arms around his neck. Getting a bit above him, I sink deeper into the kiss, scraping my tongue deep within his mouth. Hearing the groan from him is the ultimate orgasm preparation.

He carries me through the house, and I don't even open my eyes to direct him. It takes him a minute, but he finds my bedroom, all while I'm digging my fingertips into his scalp, holding him to me.

Brewer barks a few times, and I hear him following us.

Deke disengages, and then I'm flying through the air on a small scream before hitting the comfortable bed in a *poof*. He drops his body down on me as he roams every curve of my body. And I have them. Lots of them. I just can't give up pizza, not happening. From his eagerness, he has not one qualm with any of it.

"Dog," Deke says.

I watch as Brewer lifts his head, circles twice, and then finds a seat on the floor.

I run my hands over the planes of his well-toned back and remember the beautiful Angel and how it moved when he punched the bag. My nails dig in at the recollection, and he makes a low sound in his throat.

Then he knifes up so quickly I have no choice but to let him go. With his knees to bed, he strips away the shirt, tossing it haphazardly to the floor. My lips become so very dry at the sight of him I wet them, Deke following my movements. The bulge in his jeans indicates he likes this. He likes it a lot.

To entice him, I sit up and pull off my shirt then my bra, doing the same as him and tossing them to the floor.

He groans a, "Fuck me."

"That's what I plan on doin', big guy."

Deke tears at his jeans and underwear, tossing them off. I move to the button of mine, but he's suddenly there, practically tearing my clothes from my body in a rush of desire.

He grabs a foil packet from the side of the bed that I missed him tossing out and rolls it on expertly. I expect him to climb on, but he grabs my ankles and pulls me down the bed. He twists my legs, and I have no choice but to follow, ending up on my side, one leg pressed in the air.

Deke crawls on knees between my legs, lining his hard cock to my entrance. No playing around with this guy; he's had enough foreplay.

I've always wanted an adventurous sex life, trying new things and seeing what makes me and my partner tick. First, truck sex, and now this. I can see that Deke is the same way.

He slides his cock inside me, and I roll so my face is in the mattress and my hand is clutching the sheets. Like this, he's touching deep.

He holds my leg up high, his hips getting to work quickly. Each thrust has his cock stretching me deliciously. When his pelvic bone starts to hit my clit, breathing becomes difficult. When he cups my breast, squeezing it hard, my core clenches around him as I give out a cry of pleasure. The orgasm races through my body, and I swear I even feel it in my toes.

Deke doesn't stop, but he does put my leg down, positions between them, holds my knees to my chest, and unleashes. The muscles in his body contort with each of his movements, his abs flexing and arms straining. If I weren't on the cusp of another screaming orgasm, I might have been able to take a few minutes to enjoy the view.

He starts to rub hard over my clit, not stopping. The pressure is too much, and I scream his name, the word echoing off the walls.

Deke leans down, takes my mouth, and groans into it as he comes, his muscles beneath my fingertips bunching.

Holy shit. That wasn't just sex. That was some sort of out of body experience or something. Shit.

"Well, this was a hell of a surprise." We lay in my tangled sheets after coming down from seriously hard orgasms.

"Glad you think so."

I roll over. Deke's well-toned body is lying flat on

the sheets, his hand up on his head. He looks damn gorgeous.

Brewer lifts his head, looking at me, probably wanting to get up on the bed, but I give him no indication it's time for that yet.

"Didn't know you made house calls."

His lips tip up. The plane of his nose has a small crook in it, but only because I'm staring can I tell. His jaw is strong and sculpts out his face perfectly. Even the way his eyelashes lay on his cheeks is sexy as hell. I'm positive there is nothing on the man's body that isn't perfection.

"Only to bombshells."

"Bombshell, huh?"

He tips his head toward me. "Fuck yeah."

I like this. I like this way more than I should. Him in my bed, calling me a bombshell after three amazing orgasms. Yeah, I like this way too much.

"Not so bad yourself, handsome."

Brewer barks. For once, I actually forgot about him.

"Hey, boy. I'll get you treats in a little bit."

He barks in response as I lay back down on Deke. "So, what brings you back to Sumner? Assuming you left."

"Yep, now I'm back." He says nothing else, and I'm not going to prod him. He wants to talk, he'll talk. If he doesn't, he won't.

"Started at X, obviously."

"Obviously. You like it?"

"So far, so good." I want to ask, so I do. "Why are you stayin' in town?"

His brow quirks, either not liking being asked a personal question or thinking I'm nuts.

"It just seemed like you didn't want to be here before," I carry on, my mouth running away from me.

"Mom's sick, so I'm gonna be around a while."

"Oh, sorry."

"You didn't do nothin'."

"I know that, but still ..." I may not know what it's like to have a sick mom, but I do know what it means not to have one. I don't want that for anyone.

"Bombshell, it'll be good. We'll get her fixed up, then go from there."

His demeanor is so calm, but I can't tell if it's a mask or if it's fear. It can't be nonchalance because he wouldn't be back here for anything that wasn't important. At least, that's what I got from the confrontation with his father.

"You wanna talk, you know where to find me."

Leaving it alone is the best thing right now. Hell, may be the best thing we got. There's really no need for the idle chitchat after sex, but that doesn't mean I don't give a shit. It just means I'll give him space.

He runs his hands through his sexy blondish-brown hair then keeps them lodged on the top of his head. Long minutes pass as he looks up at the ceiling.

I turn from him and do the same, letting my words hang in the air.

"Cancer," he says softly, in a way I didn't know a big man like Deke could say something.

Damn.

"Sorry, Deke. How bad is it?" Personally, cancer hasn't touched my life. I've never done the research, but know a little.

"Don't know. She had tests today. Won't know the results until next week."

"So, you picked up your life and came here for your momma?"

The heart this man has is much bigger than what he shows on the outside. The hard exterior is there for a reason, but inside, there's more. Charlie was right about him.

"Yep." He rolls off to the side, planting his feet on the floor. "Alright, I'm out."

A sliver of disappointment hits me, but I mask it quickly. That's what this is—in and out. I just need to take my orgasm and run away with it.

He shared with me, even if it was a small bit. Who am I to even want to have more? I get what he gives. Just like he gets what I give.

I get off the bed and duck into the closet, pulling out a robe and wrapping it around my body. Brewer follows me. I reach down and rub his head.

Deke dresses quickly then moves through the

house like he's been here a thousand times before. He gets to the front door, dips down, and takes my lips. Then he's gone.

No comment of seeing me again.

No asking for my number.

Nothing.

But that's what the deal was. Sex. And that's what we got.

Too bad the lingering disappointment hits as I watch his truck lights disappear.

CHAPTER THIRTEEN
Deke

LOUD BANGING ON THE DOOR WAKES ME FROM A NOT SO comfortable sleep. The couch in Austyn's place is lumpy as all hell. I need my own place, like yesterday. The plan is to look later today. I left pretty much everything up in Grayson that didn't mean anything to me. The ratty couch, chair, table—all of it. It was all hand me downs because I really didn't give a shit. None of it was worth hauling down here. Mostly, I grabbed my clothes and a few other things.

My landlord was cool about me taking off, saying to leave what I didn't want and whoever rented it next would probably use it.

I still don't know if this is the right decision, but I've made my bed now, so to speak, and it's time to lay in it. If I can keep my profile down, fight when I feel the build, and otherwise keep to myself, maybe my return won't make waves. My mother is too sick for me to break her heart again.

I wonder sometimes, if they knew the truth, how things would be. Would my mother understand I never intended to hurt her? I left to save her the heartache of seeing another child lost. I wouldn't put my Ravage family through the devastation. The risk was too great, and I wouldn't be the one.

When the time comes, and she gets better, she fights this, I will face it then. For now, I have to give her hope. Consequences be damned, I'll fight beside her.

Grabbing my gun, I make my way to the door and look through the peephole. Cooper stands on the other side of it, hands at his sides, his focus on the door. Fuck. Nothing says family love like an early morning wake up call.

Unlocking the door, I slide it open, revealing my cousin. His expression is neutral, not up nor down, but his shades hide his eyes.

Cooper Cruz has seen more than his fair share of a shit hand in life, and he's always been the one to handle it all in stride. He's the kind of guy it takes a lot to rattle, and even more to read.

"Austyn's in bed," I tell him, turning back to the couch, setting the gun next to me as I sit while wiping the sleep from my eyes. I'd thought about crashing at Rylie's place—wanted to, actually—but I dropped something on her that I was surprised I did. Not talking about shit has been my thing for four years. Giving her that little bit is still disconcerting, and not in a bad way, which is confusing the fuck out of me. I needed space to sort myself.

"Not here to see her." The door clicks closed as Cooper comes to the recliner and sits down. "You're my target this morning."

Dropping my arms, I say, "Lucky me."

He rests his elbows on his knees, rubbing his hands back and forth. "Talk to me."

I'm pretty sure I gave up my quota for sharing last night to Rylie. The old feelings want to come to the surface, but I push them down. This shit has got to stop somewhere. I'm just not sure it should be with Cooper.

"Austyn's asleep. Why don't you go wake her if it's a chitchat you want?" I tell him instead of answering.

"Dammit, Deke. You gotta stop this shit. I know you're not usin', and from the sound of it, you stopped four fuckin' years ago, so answer me. Why the fuck did you stay away from your family if it wasn't to get clean?"

"I really don't want to do this." That word—family —is an acid churning deep inside me and pulsing through my veins.

"Too fuckin' bad. You need to clear this shit up so we can get on with it. Your mom's got a fuck of a fight, and we don't need all this clouding over it."

Motherfucker's right, but no way in hell he's getting everything. Not happening. Fucking hell.

"Man, look—"

"Four fuckin' years, man. You ditched fuckin' everyone. Don't you dare give me some bullshit excuse, Deke. I'm not fuckin' buyin' it."

This is exactly why I didn't come back. Coop and the Ravage MC aren't fucking stupid. But they gave me this play for some reason. Or maybe my father just gave up. That one's still out for debate. Regardless, the pieces of the puzzle need to stay scattered.

"I needed to stay clean, Coop. I got a good life up there. Job, apartment, money."

"But not your fuckin' family," he cuts in, pissing me off.

I stare at him. Tall, muscular, with light brown hair that he pulls up into a bun thing on his head. Beard that hasn't been trimmed in days. All of it added with his confidence makes him a spitting image of his father.

"Family," I huff. "I don't think this is a conversation we need to have."

"Deke, we're your family."

That word again. It calls to the demons, drawing them out.

My blood pumps a little faster, my ears hear a little clearer, my senses coming alive as my body readies. I fight the rage building.

They don't know me. They think they do, but no one does. Everything is family to them, yet they can't see what's right in front of their eyes when it comes to me. I left for family.

"You have no idea what it's like to be in your shadow. To want something so fuckin' bad you can taste it, but it's out of your reach. You have no idea the shit I've been dealt, but I deal and move the fuck on. I had to become the man I am today."

He turns fully toward me, raking his hands through his hair. "You done bein' the man *you are today*?"

Smartass.

"Fuck no," I clip, and he chuckles.

"Look, I was pissed you left. Fuck, if I get real, I was pissed you didn't see the potential in you everyone else saw. Pissed you acted like an entitled fuck. More pissed when I saw your mom cryin' because you weren't around. Pissed seein' Emery watchin' the brothers and sisters hassling each other and the look of despair every damn time crossing her face. Pissed for a long fuckin' time for a lot of fuckin' reasons."

I raise an eyebrow. "Now you're not pissed?"

"Oh, I'm pissed." To this, I feel my lip curl. "We'll work that shit out later. Right now is about family. Need to know where your head's at."

This sounds like something my father would do— let Cooper come to feel me out.

"My father send you?"

He looks up at the ceiling. "Fuck, you got your hands full with him."

Coop's been paying attention.

"Like that's somethin' I don't already know."

"You stayin'?"

I lean back on the couch and stretch my legs out in front of me. "For a while."

He crosses his leg over his knee. "That doesn't sound promising."

"It's all I can give ya. I'll be here for Mom, and that's what matters."

He adds, "And Emery."

"Fuck, I don't want to think about tellin' her this shit."

"Bet not."

"Emery tells me you got a woman."

The jackass smiles hugely. "Bristyl. Things are solid."

"Good, man."

"Hey!" Austyn chimes, coming out of the hallway in her sleep shorts and top. "What're you doin' here?"

Cooper's face softens at the sight of his sister. "Came to talk to Deke, little sis."

Austyn pushes Cooper's shoulder. "Don't call me that," she growls, but it's fake and more teasing.

"Shut it," Cooper tells her as she walks over to the couch and plops down on the other end, propping her legs up. There are so many questions that I still want to ask her, but I keep them in check.

"So, what do we owe for this wakeup call?"

Coop responds, "Havin' words."

"Bein' nice?" she asks, and I hold in a chuckle.

"Always."

"Right."

"Alright, I gotta take a leak, eat, and get over to my parents to talk to Emery. She's due in a couple hours." I rise from the couch with a stretch.

"Deke," Coop warns.

"Don't. Just don't. I get you. Appreciate you lookin' out for my mom. But that's all, Coop," I lay out for him in hopes he'll let this shit go. Those pieces need to stay scattered.

Unfortunately, I know my cousin. He doesn't detour, and even if he lets me off with this shit, he's going to look into it. I just hope he doesn't find what he's looking for.

"Not over, Deke," he says, rising from his chair with a look of concern and anger crossing his features. "Know you gotta talk to Emery. Then we're hashin' this out."

"That doesn't work for me."

"Don't give a fuck." He steps into my personal space, and my body goes on full alert.

Cooper and I didn't have the knock down fights I had with Nox when we were younger. Ours was more of a drifting away. With his build and mine so evenly matched, it'd be a fuck of a fight, not that it's my intent. I just won't back down.

"Neither do I," he challenges. "Get your fuckin' head screwed on today. We're talkin' and endin' this shit."

"You seem to have me mistaken for someone who takes orders from you. Back the fuck up," I growl, anger pumping through my veins. Even though I know he's right, know he'll push me until I talk, it's not happening.

"Guys, stop!" Austyn cries out, coming between us. Only when she pushes on my chest do I take a step back to allow her in. "This needs to stop!"

"Stay out of this, Austyn," Cooper orders.

Austyn huffs. "Right." She turns to me. "Go to the bathroom."

"Stay out of my shit, Cooper," I demand, turning around and exiting the room.

His shit is not needed, but I know it's not over. The last thing anyone needs is for Ravage to be all up in my past.

THE HOUSE IS NOW a light blue color. When I lived here, it had a tan siding with dark blue shutters. The same shutters are there, still the same color. Flowers line the outside, and the tree in the front yard where we used to have a tire swing has grown a lot.

As I pull up and into the driveway, memories assault me. Some good, some not. The main one is home. Truthfully, I like the life I built in Grayson, but it never felt like home. It was a place to live, work, and crash. Here, in the driveway, that sense of home washes over me. It's friendly and a bit unwanted.

This isn't supposed to be home anymore, but I can't fight the feeling that it is.

The door to the front swings open and Emery stands there, sees the truck, and begins a mad dash to me. Damn, she's beautiful and reminds me of our mother. Long, golden blonde hair that reaches her ass and thick as all hell. Small frame, and a face that'll have men's dicks hard. She'd better hope all those fuckers keep their dicks away from her or I'll destroy them.

I hop out of the truck and shut the door. She barrels into me, jumping up and wrapping her arms around my neck and legs around my middle. Her body shakes with quiet sobs as I clutch her tightly. That black heart inside begins to shatter. My baby sister is broken in my arms. There isn't any motherfucker's ass to kick except my own.

Kills me I did this shit to her. Even worse is the blow Mom's going to give her.

"Shhh ... It's okay."

"You're here." Her words come out as a whispered hiccup. I feel her breathing in and out on my neck, trying to calm herself.

"Yep."

"It's bad, isn't it?" Even with her body coming down from the tears, it shakes, letting me know her fear. Hate it, but it's a part of life.

"Yep."

"Shit." Her legs fall from around me, and then she takes a step back. "Still glad you're here."

I wrap my arm around her neck and pull her to my side. "Let's go in and do this."

"Yeah."

EMERY CRIES in my arms as I absorb all her pain, or at least attempt to. My mother surprisingly has held herself together well throughout. Her strength is admirable, because she must be scared as hell. But the only thing she's giving us is she's happy to have her two kids under the same roof.

If that's what she needs to hold on to right now, then so be it.

My father has stayed fairly quiet this entire time, though his disapproving glances at me come often.

That man used to be my idol. Now we can't stand to be in the same room as each other, yet we'll need to get along, at least in front of my mother. She doesn't need to worry about us, which I know she will. That's her way. The least I can do is lessen the blow and not have it in her face. Hopefully, my father can do the same.

"Okay, I'm going to make lunch, and then we're going to sit at the table and eat," my mother says, standing up.

"You don't need to be cookin' today," my father declares, and my mother shoots him a look to kill, shutting him up.

"I'm cooking for my family." When she turns and walks out of the room, my father looks at Emery and me, then follows her out.

Emery pulls away, wiping the wetness from her face and sucking in air, trying to pull herself together. "Well, this isn't good."

"She'll beat it, Emery. Gotta be strong for her and hold your shit together around her."

"Right. I'm transferring here to community college."

As much as I hate the thought, Mom will want it. "But you stay in school."

"Yeah, I will."

"Come on."

She rises, takes my hand, and pulls me out the front door, around the back, and to the old swing. This swing has been around for years and probably knows more secrets than anyone can count. I even spent my fair share of time out here, sitting and looking out over the yard. Our parents' home sits on an acre and a half with trees around it.

This swing was a calm among the storm more times than I can count. It's also a place where I'd take my hits when no one was home, making those great feelings take a turn.

Starting the drugs was a huge mistake, one that I'll never live down. Doing them here was another mistake. I tainted this place with them.

Emery sits and I follow, the wood creaking under my weight. It's old and in dire need of some care. I make a mental note to try to do that for my mom. She loves this swing, and it means a lot to her. Again, it's the least I can do. All it needs is a good scrub, some poly, and WD40.

"Are you staying for good?" Emery asks, looking out among the trees.

"Can't answer that. One day at a time."

Being here is a risk. I can only hope that he's moved on.

"Guess it's better than nothin'."

We sit out on the swing for an hour, and I learn several things about my sister's life at school. It's as I expected. Going from people all around you to no one is a difficult thing. Now, though, that the decision is made for her to come home, she's a little unsure about it. My reassurances she'll be alright get me a smile.

Lunch is tense. Sitting at the table again after four years of being absent knocks me somewhere deep. A place I've locked up for many years. Looking around at my parents and sister, though, it starts to shatter. It takes everything in me to keep it from bursting through.

Emery talks enough for everyone, telling our parents about her life and what her decisions are from this point on. My dad gets this soft look on his hard face when she talks. I'm glad she has that. She's got the whole daddy's little girl thing down pat.

Leaving isn't easy, but at five, I'm ready for a break. I drive by a couple of properties and somehow end up in Rylie's driveway.

Rylie's door opens as she walks out. Fuck, she's hot. Dynamite distraction.

Bombshell.

CHAPTER FOURTEEN
Rylie

"This is a surprise."

Deke says nothing as Brewer barks. Instead, he wraps his arm around my waist, lifting me and connecting his lips with mine. He kisses me deeply, roughly, and hard, while I hold on to the side of his head.

The door slams as he pushes us into the house, slamming my back against the wall with a thud.

When Brewer jumps up, I hear Deke snap his fingers. I look over to see Deke pointing to the floor. Brewer moves away and sits. *Good boy.*

Deke doesn't relent with me, though, and something tells me that rough is how this is going to play out. I'm totally down with that.

With one hand, he clutches my wrists and holds

them above my head. The loss of them only turning me on more as I melt into the wall. He moves his body closer, pressing me deeper into the hardness behind my back.

Our lips tear at each other, teeth crashing and breathing sparse.

Then he releases me, saying, "Clothes off now." And I kick my jeans off in a hurry, watching as he undoes his pants, not taking them all the way down before he rolls a condom on.

He brings his hands to my hips. "Hands to the wall, ass tipped up."

Brewer whines.

"Brewer, out!" Deke commands, and sure enough, little taps of his nails can be heard throughout the place.

I comply, turning around and earning me a slap on the ass that sends fire through my core. He presses my thighs together tightly, angles out my hips, then he's inside of me.

This position is acutely tight, and I try to clutch the wall, unable to get any kind of a grip. What I wouldn't give for a damn shelf or something so I could have leverage. Instead, I put my hands flat on the wall and thrust back as he comes at me, giving and taking. Same as him.

Deke must have a magic cock because I burst, falling face first into the wall, my ass tipped up, giving him an even deeper angle, which he uses to his advantage, finding his own release.

My knees begin to buckle, but he wraps his arm around my waist, lifts me, and carries me to the couch, sitting me on his lap. I note his jeans never fell all the way to the floor. That's seriously sexy.

We sit there for long moments until my brain kicks in. "Gotta go to work."

"Got it, babe." He lifts me off him, rises, and buttons his jeans.

Watching him, seeing his tight ass move, for the first time in a long time, I don't want to go to Schade's to work. I'd rather stay here and have that ass several more times.

"You at X tonight?" He looks over his shoulder, seeing me staring, and gives me a sexy as hell wink. I don't hide it, because he's hot and I don't give a shit. He's in my house and just fucked the hell out of me. If I want to stare at his ass, I will and won't be shy about it.

"Schade's."

"Schade's?"

I rise and grab my clothes, slipping my underwear on and clasping my bra. "Fight club on the outskirts."

He slips on his T-shirt. "You fightin'?"

It makes me feel good that he believes I can do so in a fight club. That shit isn't easy, and the people who go in there have balls. Not that I wouldn't. It's just not my thing.

"Nope. Security."

"Security at a fight club?" The puzzled look on his face is funny, so I smile as I slip on my jeans.

"Thought you told me you fight?"

"We don't have security."

"Schade makes bank. Runs it like an event, bringin' in people from all over. He's particular about what happens."

"You get a lot of trouble there?"

"Not too much. There's somethin' every night, but nothing I can't handle. There's a team of us."

His brows rise, and I find it cute, if that's possible to find on a man like Deke.

"Team?"

"Yep. Like I said, it's serious. You wanna come check it out?" The words come out before I realize what I'm saying, and hope flares that he'll say no. Not because I don't want him to see it. It's for the same reason I don't like Charlie there—the distraction. And Deke is a fuck of a distraction.

A pang of jealousy niggles inside me. The thought of all those women getting a take on Deke doesn't make me feel good. Some of the women there will fuck anything and everything. They'll be all over him like a fly on shit, and I'll really have to keep myself in check.

Fuck.

"Sure," he answers, and my hope dies. I can hack it,

though. Having him there and keeping an eye on the crowd, it'll be fine.

"Alright. Let me put Brewer out, and then we can grab a bite and go. You wanna ride in the Jeep?"

"I'll drive."

"I can drive."

"Do I have a dick?"

I chuckle. "Yep, pretty nice one."

"Pretty nice?"

"Yep."

He gives me a smirk, and I wonder what it would be like to get the full-on smile. The one that isn't reserved or held back. Or maybe I don't. I fear it would knock me on my ass.

"I'll drive."

"Is this some macho man thing?"

"Nope, it's just a man thing. Get used to it."

Part of me wonders if he'll be around long enough to "get used to it."

"Whatever."

DEKE OPENS the door for me to the local burger joint. As soon as we sit in a back booth, a waitress comes and takes our order.

It's a bit strange, because this is something normal.

No coming to my house in the middle of the night and fucking. Almost like a damn date.

I don't want my mind to go there. Deke doesn't come off as a dating kind of man.

"Where are you stayin'? Did you get a place?"

"Stayin' with Austyn right now. Need to find a place. Looked today, but that's the goal for tomorrow."

"Guess that means you'll be stayin' in town for a while."

"For the time bein'." His response is vague.

I need to keep in mind that he's not staying in town, so getting attached to this man in any sort of way isn't a good thing. *Sex. Keep it at sex.*

My last man, Lance, wasn't adventurous in the bedroom, but he gave decent orgasms. He was attentive to me and fixed things around my house, but there wasn't a spark. That ignition that I get when I see Deke show up at my doorstep.

The struggle to keep those thoughts separate from the "just having sex" is getting difficult, but I can do it. Keep it light. I don't want to push him away, even if it's just for a quickie. It'll all work out. It always does.

WE ENTER Schade's and see Breelyn right away. Her eyes grow wide at the sight of Deke as she looks him up from top to toe, taking in all that is him. And damn, there's a lot to take in.

"And who is this?" she asks.

"Deke."

Her gaze cuts to me. "You been hiding him?"

I smile. "Yep."

"Girl, you do not hide a piece like this."

Deke crosses his arms, no doubt not really caring for being called a piece of meat.

"We're goin' in." I make a move to do just that.

"You're talking later. Don't give a shit if I have to load you on rum. Your ass is talking," she calls out, and I give her a wave.

"Friend of yours?"

"Oh yeah. And she'll be hounding me down after work or calling me at the ass crack of dawn in the morning. Got two more close ones here, so get ready."

He shakes his head as he takes in the space, saying nothing. I wish I could get inside his head and figure out what he's thinking.

"You do whatever. I gotta get to work."

He lifts his chin as I move off.

After checking in with Schade, the team, and scoping the area, people begin to pile in. I clock Deke in the back of the place, leaning against the wall. The entire air around him screams "don't come near me and don't touch me." So far, he's been given a wide berth, but the place isn't packed yet, and it will be a crush.

The night goes smoothly, only Jackson getting kicked out so far for starting his usual shit. I haven't lost sight of Deke all night. Not to mention the women he caught the eye of. They've been circling like vultures, and every time one goes up to him, I have the severe impulse to beat the living shit out of them. Luckily, he's sent each of them away.

I know I have zero claim to the man, but I still don't like it.

Three fights down when the last one takes the cage up in the center. The room is electric, everyone pumped from watching the first three. It seems that the last one always has more of a pump than the first. Could be all the alcohol helping that out. Schade makes a killing on booze. No way he'd ever stop that shit.

The roar of the crowd and the sounds from the fighters fill the room. Weeding through the people, my body is pushed and pulled. Some make a few grabs, but mostly, I ignore them. That's what they want—attention. I don't give it, they get the point.

A hand grabs my arm, turning me. Another grabs my pussy as lips come down on mine. I break away and kick the guy in the gut, pushing him into the crowd. Good-looking man with dark jeans, a T-shirt, and dark hair, but asshole for thinking he can grab, kiss, and touch me.

Just as I make my way over to him, ready to show him exactly what pisses me off, out of the corner of my eye, I see Deke storming through, pushing people if needs be. When I say storm, I mean, literally everyone in his path moves feet away from him, noting the anger pulsing off him. He is ready to explode.

The guy only has eyes for me as he comes back at me, but Deke catches him by the throat. His arm strains as he clenches the man, lifting him clean off the floor.

Holy shit!

The guy who touched me kicks his legs and tugs at Deke's hand, trying to free himself. But with the grip Deke has, it'll take a hell of a lot more than that to get him loose.

The strength Deke has is something I'm in awe of. It's as if he's a mix of the Hulk and the Rock or something. It's the clear, controlled rage, though, that's really getting me. It's there, but he has it in check. He has a pulse on exactly what he's doing and each action. It makes me wonder what he's like in the ring.

I move up to his side so he can see me out of the corner of his eye.

"Deke, let him go."

Deke stares down at the man who's clearly about

ready to piss his pants. The guy may be aggressive to women, but to men, he's a pussy.

Deke pulls the guy to within a foot of his face and growls, "Fuckin' touch her again, I'll end you." With that warning, he throws the guy, knocking several people over in the process. Fuck, this isn't going to be good.

"Boys!" I call in, but my guys are already there, helping to settle everyone.

Deke's eyes don't leave the man on the floor until I step into his vision. He tags me around my waist, pulling me to his hard body, bringing his lips down on mine, hard and rough. I take it because I want it.

He breaks away, looking down at me. "I'm fuckin' you, no one fuckin' touches you." He sets me back, turns to look at the crowd around us, then stalks back to the back of the room.

Holy shit. Did that just happen?

Arousal hits me between my legs. I have to admit, that was the hottest thing any man has ever done for me. It'll piss Schade off, but fuck me.

"WHAT THE FUCK IS THIS? Bring your boyfriend to work night?" Schade practically yells at me as I enter his office. "Fuck, Rylie! What was that?"

Deke did start a fuck of a fight with all the people he knocked down when he threw that asshole who touched me. The crowd didn't go after him, though. They went after the asshole. We ended up having to protect his ass and carry him out of the place. He'll be feeling it tomorrow, but that's his own damn fault. It took a while before we got everything under control. I didn't mind.

The entire time, I kept thinking about how ironic it was that I was contemplating taking off a few of the women's heads, when Deke was thinking the same thing. Difference is, he acted and didn't give a fuck about anything but his task.

"We took care of it."

"Yeah. Damn, I hate messes." He breathes out. "He your man?"

Schade's taken care of me for the past three years. He's not one of my girls, by any means, but he keeps tabs on me, like on who I date, and has given his opinion on several occasions. Including, Lance.

Schade didn't like him at all. Now I know why.

"I'm seein' him."

Schade crosses his arms. "He's a fuckin' tank."

I smirk, knowing he's damn rock-hard everywhere on his body. "Yeah, he is."

"He a fighter?"

"Yeah, he was back home." The instant the words leave my lips, I know what his next will be.

"You bring him to me this week. We need to talk."

"About fighting or kickin' a guy's ass."

A sly smirk comes across his face. "Both."

"Don't give me shit. You're really not pissed about Deke grabbing the guy? What's this?"

"Know him. Or, more to the point, know his old man. He comes in here, I don't need the Ravage MC breathin' down my neck. Do I want him in the ring? Fuck yeah. Around here, Gavelson is a big name and will attract a crowd. Do I want that MC involved? Fuck no. That's what we need to discuss."

Know him. There's something about that I don't like. Maybe I'm just curious of what he knows.

On a shrug, I reply, "I'll relay the message. But gotta tell ya, Schade, he's not much for anyone 'telling' him anything, so be warned."

"Don't you worry. I know how to handle him."

To that, I smile. "We shall see."

Schade gives me my cut, I meet Deke by his truck, and then we take off.

"I should be pissed at you," I tell him when he doesn't say much on the drive back to my place.

"Be what ya want," he responds. "But I'm tellin' ya, anyone touches ya, I'll rip their limbs from their body."

A shiver goes down my spine. I have no doubt the man could do it.

"That's pretty hot, Deke."

"Thought you were pissed."

I unbuckle my seatbelt then lean over the console. "I said I should be. Instead, I'm horny as hell." I reach down and unbutton his jeans. He lifts his hips just a bit, enough for me to get his cock out.

"That right," he grunts as I squeeze him hard.

"Yeah."

Sticking my tongue out, I lick from the base all the way to the tip, letting the taste of him sear into my brain. Stroking the mushroom tip of his cock, then dipping into the small slit, I work him up and down. Over and over, I torture him, never putting his cock between my lips, only using my tongue.

Deke laces his fingers through my hair, tightening and pulling. It makes me smile around his cock. Then he shifts his hips up, wanting more.

"Suck my cock, Rylie," he orders.

Instead of complying, I wrap my lips around the sides of his cock and move them up and down, feeling every ridge and vein. The center console digs into my chest, but the pain is ignored.

He growls low, his grip getting even tighter. I watch as his abs flex beneath his shirt.

Some women think sucking cock is degrading, that it makes them less of a woman or gives them a loss of control. Not me. This is the most powerful I feel, being able to bring a man to his knees just by tongue, lips, and hands. Having his body quiver and shake with each movement I make, wanting more and beginning to lose control.

The grunts and groans coming from his lips, and the way his muscles contract, tell me just how much he likes what I'm doing. Yes, this is powerful.

Finally needing more, I engulf him, wrapping him in the wet warmth.

"Fuck …" he groans as his thigh muscles tense, and I feel an acceleration in the truck's speed. See, power.

At his groan, I unleash, sucking, stroking, licking all in quick, rapid successions.

The truck makes a turn as Deke growls again, his cock growing thicker in my hand, and the pulse of the vein at the bottom of it starting to thump hard.

Taking him deeper, so deep I have to control my gag reflex, the truck brakes hard and my head bumps the wheel, but I recover quickly.

The truck is thrown into park, and then Deke moves his other hand to my head and begins thrusting his hips up. I don't relent, my already wet panties dampening from Deke's display.

"Fuck!" he roars, shoving his hips up and coming inside my mouth. I suck and swallow as his taste coats my mouth.

His body falls into the seat, and only then do I clean him up and pull off him.

With a smile on my face, I start to move back to my seat, but am stopped when lips crash to mine. More of his taste mingles inside me, and now it's me groaning into his mouth.

He rips his lips away. "House, bed, clothes off," he orders, letting me go and knifing out of the truck like he's on a fucking mission.

I comply after letting Brewer out and giving him his rub down, because this mission is more than likely going to come with several orgasms.

We make quick work of getting down to business, his lips on me, fingers in me. All of it happening so fast I can't even remember entering the house. The passion and desire have taken over, consuming me with every bit of myself.

I realize pretty fucking quickly how much Deke likes his cock sucked and make a mental note to do it more often.

CHAPTER FIFTEEN
Deke

DAMN, THAT WOMAN CAN SUCK. FUCKING DEEP-throated me, and I'm not a small man. Even lying here after two orgasms myself, and countless for her, my cock twitches at the thought of being inside her wet heat again.

Rylie's breathing is coming hard and fast as she lies next to me, her hair spread out on my arm that's under her neck. We stare at the ceiling, no one talking, yet not needing to. Comfortable silence. Peace. Something I didn't think was possible during the shit-storm that is my life.

"Stay with me," she whispers, still looking above her and not at me, like she's afraid of what my answer or reaction will be to those words.

When I say nothing after a moment, she rolls off to the side.

"Never mind. Shouldn't have—"

I wrap my arm around her waist and pull her back onto the bed, cutting off her words. She gives a small cry in surprise.

"Ya know, you should really let a man talk before you start jumpin' to conclusions."

Her body tenses, but she says nothing.

"Better havin' your tight ass against me while I sleep instead of that lumpy-ass couch." I kiss the top of her head. "Sure, babe."

She lets out a deep breath and nestles her ass into my crotch, reminding me I need to take off the condom. I give her a squeeze.

"Gotta get this off."

"Okay."

I roll off, do my business, come back, and toss the covers over the both of us. Never knew I liked holding a woman in my arms while I slept. Tonight proves that I do.

Brewer jumps on the bed, shaking it.

"Come here, boy," Rylie calls, and I feel the dog lie down on the other side of her. Fine by me.

LOUD BANGING and a doorbell going off wakes me from the most peaceful damn sleep I've had in more years than I can count. Two days in a fucking row I've been woken up by this shit. This had better not be Coop, or I'll lay his ass out.

Brewer barks, obviously not liking whoever is waking us, either.

Rylie groans, rolling over. "Who the fuck is here?"

"That'd be my question, babe."

"Right. Brewer, chill."

When she throws the covers off her, I wrap her in my arms. Her naked body presses to mine, and my cock instantly hardens. Damn, this woman undoes me.

"Stay here. I'll take care of it."

"You sure?"

I kiss her temple. "Yeah."

After giving her a squeeze and finding my jeans, I make my way to the door that whoever is behind is making a hell of a damn noise. In all the action last night, I left my gun in the truck. Great damn place for it. Brewer is hot on my heels.

Looking through the peephole, I see an older woman standing there with light brown hair that's cut super short and curled tight against her scalp. She's wearing a light blue skirt that looks like a fabric quilt. She squints at the peephole like she knows I'm looking through it.

"Rylie!" the woman yells, just as I open the door. She halts, taking me in.

"Somethin' I can help you with?" I ask as the dog barks twice.

"Who are you?" she clips, turning her nose up at me.

I get enough of that shit from my so-called family, I won't eat hers, too.

"Aunt Beatrice?" Rylie asks, coming behind me.

"Floozy. Knew you were. This proves it. Some man opening the door and you in nothing but a T-shirt."

"Nice to see you, too," Rylie clips. "What do you want?"

"Told you I was short this month—"

"And I told you, I wasn't givin' you shit. Now you show up at my house?"

"After all that I did for you, you owe me," the aunt growls low.

Rylie moves in front of me quickly, and Brewer gets by her side with a growl of his own. I really fucking like that dog.

"Done for me? Are you fuckin' kidding me? You did shit for me. I lived on the fuckin' streets because you didn't want anything to do with me. You hate me. You've told me time and time again. Hell, my mother liked everyone, but you. I told you last time you called to forget my number. Now you forget where I live. I don't want to hear from you ever again."

"How dare you say such things about my sister! She loved me!"

Rylie chuckles. "Yeah, she loved you, but she damn sure didn't like your ass."

"You ungrateful—"

"Me? I'm ungrateful? You're the one who took all of my parents' money and squandered it away."

"I used it to take care of you."

"What, feeding me? Nope. Did that myself. Buyin' me clothes? Nope. Did that myself, too. You haven't done a damn thing for me my entire life. I had no choice but to go with you. Now I do, and I don't want you in my life anymore." The entire time, she keeps her voice eerily calm.

"You know who I am and what I can do," the woman threatens.

Personally, I thought the woman was full of shit, spouting crazy at Rylie. The way she said that, though, sends me on alert.

"And you know who I am. Don't fuckin' threaten me. I'll end you."

Rylie steps back from the door, slamming it, and then locking it. Brewer once again is at her side. She doesn't meet my eyes as she moves to the living room and stands behind one of her chairs. She plants her fists in the soft cushion at the top while her head is bowed, looking at them. She has a slight tremble to her body, but it doesn't come off as fear. No, it comes off as rage. Full-blown rage.

I totally get what she feels right now, so I decide my

best bet is to let her have this moment. I toss my ass down on the couch, throw my arm over my eyes, and wait.

It doesn't take long.

"That fuckin' bitch. I need to burn her to the ground." Rylie hits the chair once and breathes out. "Fuck, I hate her."

I don't talk, just let her get whatever she needs out. This is what I would need, along with a punching bag.

It takes her several beats before she blows out, "I'll make breakfast." Then she leaves me in the living room.

"You really don't need to move out, Deke," Austyn says as I gather my bag of shit. I put most of it in a storage unit in town, not wanting shit to get stolen out of the back of my truck. I don't have a lot, but still, what's mine is mine. Come to find out the Ravage MC owns it, which is something new.

"Need my own space."

"I kinda like having you here," she says shyly.

"I'm still around."

"You haven't slept here in, like, four nights, Deke."

Very true, because I've been at Rylie's. But she doesn't need to know that.

There is an insecurity in her eyes I don't like. I also know, as much as she wants me to stay, I can't.

"Thanks, kid. You got your head screwed on straight after what happened?"

She stills at my comment, eyes going wide, obviously not expecting me to bring that up. Too fuckin' bad.

"I'm fine, Deke. No more talking about that. Ever."

"You ever need to, I'm around."

"Right."

She gives me a hug, and I reciprocate before pulling away and heading to my new place. It's not anything fancy, but it's got a bedroom, which is more than my old place had. Not to mention the living room is bigger and could fit a pull-out couch. I hate fucking shopping, but I'll scratch that off my agenda later today.

My cell rings, and I see the display says, *Cruz calling*. Fuck. I should let it go to voicemail, but he's left me alone for the most part.

"Yeah."

"Clubhouse, one hour." The line disconnects.

Great, I'm being fucking summoned. Such bullshit. Then why I find myself going an hour later is up for debate. Instincts, I suppose.

Entering the clubhouse, Cruz greets me by lifting his chin, turning, then walking down the hallway. I look for my father, but don't see him anywhere. Either he's waiting for me in Cruz's office or this is a one-on-one show.

Instead of my father, Cooper stands there with his hip against the wall, arms crossed over his chest, his eyes focused on me as I lift my chin.

The door behind me closes.

Cruz doesn't waste time. "Hear you're good with cars and bikes. Want you workin' in the shop."

Ravage owns Banner Automotive, which is on the clubhouse property. When I was a kid, my father would bring me there and teach me. We'd work together on cars, bikes, and trucks. It's where I learned most of what I know. Good times were had in that shop. Now, though, I'm not interested.

"No."

I turn to move, considering this is all they wanted. I'm not getting sucked into the Ravage MC by working for them.

"Stop," Cruz commands, deep and authoritative, just like when Coop and I used to get into trouble back in the day.

Cooper rounds the chairs in front of the desk and comes toward me, saying nothing.

"Deke, you need to get over whatever shit you're carrying around. This is family. We're two men down and need the help. You're in town, you're good."

"What makes you think for one second that I want to come and work for Ravage?"

Cruz crosses his arms. "Need you back in the fold."

"Is that right? Then why isn't my ol' man here? Right, because he doesn't want me anywhere near here. Only puttin' up with me because of Mom. You think I want to be a part of that shit?"

"You always wanted to be part of the club," Cooper says. "You gonna say that's changed? It's a part of you, in your blood, and who you are—who we are."

"No shit? You know this. We fuckin' talked about it. It's nothin' new. But shit's changed. I've changed."

"Have no doubt you've changed," Cruz says, his eyes suddenly very aware. "You weren't ready then. Can't deny that shit. Now, you are."

"Just like that?" I snap my finger in the air. "You know jack shit about me. How the fuck do you know I'm ready? I call bullshit."

"You'd be smart, because you have a lot to prove," Cruz responds, leaning his ass against his desk and crossing his ankles in front of him. "This is your first step. You ready to take it?"

Damn, this is huge.

A war wages inside of me. For four years, I've fought this, and now it's all coming back in an explosion.

"What makes you think I'm even stayin' after this shit is out of my mom?"

"Because, you left her once and missed four years.

She beats this shit, you're not gonna waste any more time. Not only that, I hear you have a girl here."

This catches my attention. I should've known they'd have someone digging into me. Wouldn't surprise me if it was Cooper himself.

"Leave Rylie out of this shit," I growl, not liking her name brought up in any of this.

"Got no problem with her. She fuckin' works for us, Deke. Just know you've got somethin'. Don't see you wantin' to jump ship on your mother and her any time soon."

I don't, but fuck. Getting back in the club life is the unknown. This can't be an option.

Shit, can it?

"Know you got a shitload of cash in the bank and probably don't need to work."

I growl again, anger bubbling in my veins. "Stay out of my shit."

Cruz chuckles. "Nah, it's better this way. But we need you here. Starting as soon as possible."

"Since you checked into shit, you know how much I make."

"Yep, and you'll be compensated the same."

Fuck me.

"I'll think about it."

"No isn't an option. It's family, Deke," Cruz says, dipping his chin.

I take it as my exit. I don't look back as I get the fuck out of there. I need a drive and a heavy bag.

Fuck, I'm getting sucked back into the Ravage MC. This is unexpected.

"YOU DON'T HAVE to do this," Rylie says from the passenger side of my truck.

After leaving the clubhouse and thinking, the anger inside me started to flow over like hot lava. I tried going to the gym and beating it out of the bag, but it didn't help. That's where I saw Rylie and took her up on the offer to go see her guy Schade at the fight club. I need to get this aggression out and settle down the demons inside of me.

Fuck, this is bad. Really bad.

Crawling out of an unknown bed, the weight of the night hits me like a concrete block, forcing me to sink below the surface of the water.

I didn't use. I know I fucking didn't, yet the drug is in my body, surging through my veins, almost out of my system.

I've felt this enough times to know. If only I could figure out why I feel this shit.

I made a vow to myself after the second stint in rehab that I wouldn't touch the stuff, no matter what, I was going to pull myself together. For one week, I've been able to hack it and stay strong.

Last night, some guys from school wanted to go out. Nothing exciting, just some racing down on the dirt on Corner Road. We were just going to watch, and that was cool.

It wasn't until much later that he made his appearance, one I couldn't avoid. No matter where I turned, he was there. I even told the guys I needed to head out. They were with me, but they needed to make their rounds before we could go. They were tight with most of the people there.

If I would've stayed in my place and not left, I wouldn't have seen it. I wouldn't have been knocked out. And I wouldn't be feeling like I've been run over by a bus this morning. I wouldn't have this craving so fiercely.

The problem with addiction is it never ends with just one hit. Withdrawal is hell. This feeling, though ... having shit in my system, I swear I didn't put it there. It's a loss of all control.

I drag my ass to my buddy's and clean up before I head home. I need to talk to my dad. He's the only one who can tell me what to do and how to play this. I know I'm in trouble, because that asshole won't stop. His threats ring through my ears.

Pulling up to my house, I look in the mirror. My eyes have turned back to white, but bags show how exhausted I am. I hope like hell he can't tell I was on anything last night.

The door swings open as I make my way up and my father stands there with his arms crossed.

"Where the fuck have you been?"

Damn, he's already pissed. Regardless, I need to get through to him.

"Jon's," *I answer, entering the house. The door slams behind me.*

"See you're up to your old shit again," *he clips as I turn and face him in the entryway of my childhood home.*

I rush, "It's not that, Dad. I need to talk to you."

"Fucking little shit! I can't believe you!" *His voice is so loud the neighbors will be eating this shit up.* "Kept your mom up all fuckin' night, and not a care in the world to what your shit does to her. Ungrateful shit."

"It's not what you—"

My father steps forward, getting in my face. "One time you go out, and you're on that shit again. Knew I shoulda locked your ass down. But your mother wanted to give you a chance. She always wants to give you another chance. She ends up wide awake and worried. Now you've fucked it all up. You fucking disgust me!" *he roars, and I take a step back.*

"Dad ..." *I try again, but he laughs.*

"You're done. I don't want to hear shit from you." *The vein in his neck pulses, and he clenches his fists, no doubt wanting to knock some sense in me. But he's wrong, and he won't listen. He's too far gone. Too far pissed off at me.*

There is no way he will believe me. I know what I need to do. He's left me no other choice.

What we had is gone.

Fighting another person is the only way to beat back the anger. Pounding into flesh, hearing the grunts of a man taking my blows, it's a reminder I'm in control.

Being part of that club was what I desired for so many years. Then, when I left, I never thought I'd be tossed back into the fold.

I'm no moron. If I take this job at the garage, I'm in. Also, there'll be payback for the way I left. There'll be consequences for all of that. Plus, I'll have to prove myself repeatedly until they get the me I am now. It seems like a fuck of a lot of work for your family to accept you.

I just need to clear my head of everything warring inside of it. Then maybe I'll be able to find some calm.

"Need to. Tonight."

"You want to talk about it?" she asks.

"Not now."

She turns back toward the window. I can see that I've let her down by not talking to her, but I'm just not there.

The meeting takes all of ten minutes. I tell the man I'll do the fight for free. The way Rylie sounded, the man was afraid of the club coming into play, but he didn't have any qualms after the word free came from my lips.

Rylie tapes me up as the crowd goes wild. They don't know me, but some obviously remember me from the other night. Fine by me.

The guy is about the same size as me, with fire breathing in his eyes. It doesn't matter, because I don't see him after the bell goes off. Instead, a red haze fills my vision, and I let loose.

CHAPTER SIXTEEN
Rylie

I CAN'T HELP WATCHING, MY EYES GLUED TO THE CAGE and not the crowd for once.

Blow after blow, Deke demonstrates how much power is inside of him. Meanwhile, all his opponent can do is try to fight back, giving Deke a dance that he pummels through, not once missing a beat. By the look in his eye and his cocky smirk, this is exactly what Deke wants from him.

The two men go at it hard. Deke has blood coming from his head and lip, but he doesn't stop. It's as if something breaks inside of Deke as he unleashes, and everything before this moment was just for play.

The power he had before is more now. A lot more. Blow after blow, the man is unable to block. Shots to the temple, and repeat. Deke is like a machine.

The guy falls to the ground hard, hitting his head,

but Deke doesn't stop. His rage continues to burn. It's not until the "ref" calls it when the other man passes out that Deke pulls away. His breathing is heavy, and it's sexy as all hell.

I'm a bit worried about him. Whatever happened today, it sent him somewhere deep within himself.

I don't fear him. I just worry.

Deke climbs out of the cage, his intense gaze coming to me. He wraps his arm around my neck, then pulls me through the crowd, his sweaty body next to mine. I follow, knowing I'm working, but not giving a shit. Whatever's going on with him is deep, and he obviously needs me.

Then Deke stills, halting our steps. I look up at him and see he's staring into the crowd, eyes cut into slits. Following his gaze, I see a man with longish black hair, rimmed glasses, and a lean build. He raises his can of beer to Deke like he knows him, then takes a drink.

Deke becomes unstuck and pushes our way through the crowd and out of the building to the truck.

"Get in," he orders.

"Deke, I'm working."

"Don't give a fuck. You're not stayin' there."

"Why?"

"Just get in the truck. I'll explain later."

Schade's going to be pissed at me, but I climb into the truck. Then Deke takes off like a shot.

We pull up to his apartment and move inside

quickly. I've never been the woman who follows a man. Except, with Deke, there has never been a single moment when I didn't feel like I couldn't go into the depths of Hell safely beside him. It's scary, yet it's this connection that has me craving more.

"Give me a few," he says before moving out of the room. Then I hear the shower turn on.

Today has seriously been interesting with Deke.

He only has a chair so far, so I plop my ass in it and wait.

He comes out with a towel wrapped around his sexy as fuck body, water still beading off him. His hair is a wet mess on top of his head, completing the gorgeous look.

Fuck. No man should be that hot.

Controlling myself, I ask, "Feel better?"

"The guy at the back with the dark hair? Know you saw him. He come there a lot?"

"Nope. First time I've ever seen him."

"Fuck." He runs his hands through his hair, water splashing to the carpet.

"Who is he, and how do you know him?"

He moves to me, lifts me, then sets me down on his lap. The back of my clothes get wet from him. My only wish is it would cool my libido down, but it doesn't.

"Long fuckin' story. Just stay away from him."

"Deke, please talk to me."

He wraps his arms around my body, and we sit

there for a while, my head resting on his wet chest, his chin on top of my hair. His heartbeat is calm, helping to do the same for me.

"It's just a ghost coming back from the past."

I so badly want him to open up to me. He has no idea how much I want this. He says nothing, though, just holds me in his arms. Time seems to tick by in slow motion. Then, he finally speaks.

"When I was sixteen, I got hooked on heroin."

I say nothing. If he's going to share, I'm not fucking that up. We all have ghosts of our past, and he's not on the stuff anymore, so he kicked it somehow. This is a good thing.

"The guy you saw tonight is a dealer, high up on the food chain. My dealer, he's pissed I'm back home because I'm not supposed to be." His head falls back to the cushion of the chair. "I shoulda kept a lower profile."

"Are you scared of him?"

"Me, no. What he can do to people I give a shit about, fuck yeah."

I lift my head. "You're gonna have to help me out here, Deke. Trying to get all of this, but you're gonna need to spell this out more."

"Fuck, Ry. I should just take you home."

The words settle like a rock in my gut because there's a finality to them. One I don't like one damn bit. He's pushing me away, not letting me in. Maybe he thinks he's going to protect me, but I'm in this shit. There's no going back. Furthermore, I don't want out. I care for this man, and he needs a place to release all this shit he's carrying around.

"No. Talk to me. He already saw us together. There's no going back from that."

He runs his hand through his hair. "Fuck."

At least he gets where I'm coming from. If that asshole is dangerous, I need the information. He saw Deke and me tonight. If he's there for Deke, then he could use me to get to him. The way of the world is fucked up, but I'm not a dumb bitch.

He's quiet, and it drags on for a while.

I lift up and see his face is pained, like he's reliving a part of his life that he never wanted to. One that made him into the man he is today. Not that it's bad, but whatever it is, pains him horribly.

He presses my head back down to his chest, resting his chin on top of it. "After my second stint in rehab, I was clean for a week."

I try my damnedest to keep my breathing steady, both happy and unsure about what I'm going to hear, but knowing it's heavy as hell.

"Went out with my guys. While I was there, I saw JK kill a kid about seventeen-years-old. He saw me, caught me, beat me, and drugged me. Threatened to hook Emery, Austyn, and Nox on the shit. Make it stronger for them. Force it on them if he had to. Told me the only reason he wasn't killin' me was because of my father. Knew who he was, what he stood for. Said when I was eighteen, I had to get the hell out of Sumner or he'd fuck with all of them. I disappear, he'd stay away."

There are a lot of questions I have about this scenario, so when he doesn't continue, I nail him with one.

"Why didn't you go to your father?"

He gives a slight chuckle, but there's no humor in it. "Tried. Old man wouldn't listen. Told me I was worthless. He and I have a lot of bad blood, and it's never been cleaned. He doesn't want it to be. I had a few months before I turned eighteen. I went to my aunt Princess, had her start to train me. Went to Charlie's. Started there every day and bided my time."

"How did you know this JK guy'd follow through? I mean, not give your sister anything."

He sighs. "Didn't, but I was young, a fuckin' addict, and knew if I didn't leave, he'd find me and fill me up with the drug again, because the best way to keep me doin' what he wanted while I was in Sumner was to keep me doped up. Knew he didn't want me around because I was a witness. Somethin' told me he wouldn't fuck with Emery, Austyn, and Nox because that would be too coincidental in life—all four of us gettin' hooked on the same shit. Would put him under radar. Ravage's radar is the last place he wants to be."

My brain works overtime with the pieces of the puzzle.

"You don't think the MC went looking for this guy?"

"Don't know. Never asked because I was gone. Started a new life. By the time I got my head sorted, there was no reason for me to come back."

"How do you know they didn't?"

"Talked to my sister a lot. Knew everyone was good because she woulda told me that shit right out. Kept tabs, but didn't keep tabs."

"So, you left to protect them?"

He breathes in deep and lets it out. "That was my thoughts then."

"And now?"

"Fuck if I know. Part of me is pissed at myself for not making my father listen to me or going to Cruz. But I can't go back in time, and I can't change shit."

I shift a bit in his hold. "Why do you think he was there tonight?"

"Warning."

Raising up, I look in his eyes. "He must have a death wish. The man I saw in the ring tonight will wipe the floor with him."

He gives me a squeeze. "I can and will. It's the unknown, and he is an unknown. He goes near anyone I care about, I'll destroy him."

My heart is running a damn marathon, trying to get out of my chest. I understand now what this man has been through for the past few years. I break for him, knowing what he gave up—the family that he obviously cares for deeply, and a mother who always had his back.

Time is something we can never get back. No matter what bargains we try to make, once time is gone ... it's gone.

Deke missed years with his mother, sister, and family. From the pain in his eyes, he knows it now. With his momma sick and sister home, I have no doubt that Deke will take care of this JK.

To leave everything you know, thinking you're protecting the ones you care about, takes a strong man. He wasn't really a man then, but his actions were of one. Sometimes in life, we have to grow up faster than we ever wanted to. Deke did it his way. I did it mine. It's like two vines that grew and finally met.

I'm angry with his father. I don't really know the man, have only met him a couple of times, but I did see the scene play out with Deke. That man has no idea what he did—the consequences of his actions that spun his son out and forced him to leave with no other option.

Deke's right; he should have gone to Cruz and told him exactly what was happening. Not only that, those men would've protected the kids in that club. I've seen them with the younger ones. They are fierce. Hell, the way Princess was with Austyn—fierce.

I know what it feels like to not have a choice. I didn't have one when my parents were taken from me. One day my life was great. The next, gone.

My one wish is that Deke's father sees the error of his ways before it's too late. I doubt, even now, Deke will go to GT and talk to him. That bridge has been burned, and building it back up is a job that I'm sure won't come easy.

"What's the plan?"

He lets out a heavy breath, causing both of our bodies to move with it. "Cooper. He came to me the other day, wanting to talk. I'll lay this shit on him."

"Are you tight with him?"

"Was … at one time. We have stuff to work out, but he'll listen, and he'll take it in. I'll take out JK if I need to, but having Coop at my back will be better than going at it alone."

This, I'm happy for. Deke can handle himself, but this man is dangerous on many levels. Deke said he was a big player back when he was hooked on the stuff. There's no doubt he's even higher up now, because that's what these assholes do—keep moving up until they control pretty much everything around them.

I have a couple of guys who owe me. It's time to call in that marker for information on JK.

"What can I do for you?"

His arms tighten around me, and his cock stirs

under my thigh. Deke's mouth comes to my neck. "I've got somethin' you can do."

Deke lifts me as if I weigh nothing, and then my back hits the floor. He comes down on me, but veers away from my lips, attacking my neck with a vengeance. He grips my ass hard.

With my neck arched, he has better access and takes advantage of it, his teeth nipping, lips sucking. He finds the place right below my ear and spends his time there, all the while my body catches fire and I grind my hips against his hard length.

I reach down to his ass, pushing the towel the rest of the way off of him. In this moment, I wish I had razors for nails so I could sheer my clothes off and have skin to skin contact with him.

His hand now at my breast, he finds my nipple through the fabric, giving it a pinch then a rub. My back arches off the bed, and a soft cry leaves my lips.

I push on his chest hard, garnering his attention. "Back," I order, to which he chuckles.

"You seem to forget who's in charge here."

I narrow my passion-filled eyes. "Back, now."

On a smile, he rolls us over, and I make quick work of removing my clothes.

Straddling him, his hard body beneath me, I dampen. He is absolutely the most gorgeous man I've ever had the pleasure of having under me, on me, or in me.

I slink up his body, his hands on my hips, as I leave kisses along his chest and neck before hitting his lips.

"Time for me to ride," I taunt.

His crystal blue eyes penetrate me. "Get to it." He reaches over to the table, grabs a condom, and hands it to me.

Moving down his body, I take his cock in my mouth, wrapping him up tight and giving a suck. His hips jerk and hands come to my hair. I take him in deeper, emitting a deep, guttural groan from him. Only then do I lift off and wrap him in the rubber.

Back to straddling him, his cock needs no coaxing as I make my way down and he plants himself deeply inside me. Taking a moment to just feel his hardness inside of me, I close my eyes and stick it to memory. This feeling. This connection. This ... everything.

He grips my hips hard, pulling me back to him.

"Baby, ride my cock," he orders.

On a sexy smile, I comply, using my thigh muscles to lift and lower repeatedly. The pressure inside builds. My hands unconsciously find my tits, squeezing them and pulling at the nipples, adding to the sensations already building inside me.

Deke's hips buck up, meeting mine, pressing his cock deeper and hitting inside of me hard. I cry out from the surprise of how far he can reach.

He pulls me down to him, wrapping his arms around my back and stilling my movements. Then he bends his knees, feet to the bed, and his hips take over, fast, hard, and desperate.

I can't move. I can only take what he gives me as he repeatedly thrusts into my body. Each scrape sends me higher and higher until the white rush of the orgasm has me screaming into his neck as a rush filters through every part of my body, including my toes.

Deke doesn't let me come down. Instead, he flips us and fucks me until I can't move, my limbs and arms feeling like sated jelly.

When he comes, his body strains on a grunt, all his muscles growing taut. He closes his eyes and swings his head back in the sexiest way. Gasping, he then falls off to the side of me, pulling me to him. I curl up, resting my head on his heaving chest.

"Fuck, you're amazing."

To this, I smile.

CHAPTER SEVENTEEN
Deke

MOM'S FACE IS SUNKEN IN, AND SHE HAS DEEP BAGS under her eyes. Her face is so pale, ridding me of the sunshine that she always gives. She sips the soup with trembling hands from a coffee cup. She had chemo today. A drug they put in one's body that's more toxic than the cancer trying to take over her. But they need something strong to kick it, and this time, the drugs are hitting hard.

The first round she went through didn't have this effect on her. The doctors said that would happen. It doesn't mean I have to like it.

This second round is taking its toll. These past few weeks have been up and down, and I hate this for her.

Her blonde hair is falling out—her reminder she's fighting to stay here for my sister and myself.

We've taken turns sitting with her, but I've taken over for my sister many times because she loses her battle on fighting back the sadness and tears. I get it, and I do it without her asking.

My father is a fucking mess. Not only am I in his house, but the love of his life is battling something he has no control over. One of the traits I got from him— the control—except mine came a little later in life.

"How's your woman?" my mother asks, setting down the mug like it's a lead weight, too heavy to hold a second longer.

"Good, Ma."

When she shifts on the bed, I dart up, removing the tray that was holding her food and setting it on the dresser.

"She good for you?"

In a way I didn't even know was possible.

If I never came back to this place, I wouldn't have landed in a bed next to a fucking bombshell like her. It's not just looks, either. It's her. Every damn thing about her. She listens when I need to talk. Talks when I need her to bounce me out of the thoughts in my head. She's strong as all hell and can hold her own. The only thing I've noticed about her that even slightly irks me is she shifts a lot in bed. Once I learned that pinning her down with my body stops that, there hasn't been any problems.

Hell, me laying all that shit on her, spilling my fucking guts wide open for her, she took it, held it, and let me keep going. Then she fucking asked me what she could do for me. Giving her my past, letting her have that, I knew in my gut she could take it. She didn't cower away when I told her I watched someone get murdered, because she's a woman who can hack it.

"Yeah, she is," I say, coming back to sit on the recliner next to the bed. "You'll like her." And she would. Rylie is damn likeable.

"I met her briefly. Princess says that she 'kicks ass'." My mother gives a small smile that doesn't reach her eyes in that twinkling way she does. "Said she trusts Rylie with more than the old guy. Says she's a good woman, and that's what I want for you, sweetheart. I want you to have someone you can rely on."

The tone of her words takes on a different meaning that is not lost on me one bit.

"You're fightin' this, Mom."

She reaches out and grasps my hand, giving it a squeeze. "Damn straight. Doesn't mean I don't want a good woman at your back, Deacon."

I feel the damn tickle come to the back of my throat, and I fight to keep my emotions in check. "I'm good, Ma. You worry about getting better, not me."

"I've always worried about you. Not a single moment of my life that I've had you on this planet have

I not worried about you. When you're a parent, you'll know." A cloud drifts over her eyes, more than likely imagining what life would be like if she never met her grandkids. Fuck, I don't even know if I want kids at this point.

"Get some rest. It's the best thing for ya right now."

She yawns. "It's hard because, with you close, I just want to stay awake and know it's not a trick ... that you're really here."

That ball in my stomach falls hard in my gut. Time. So much time lost. Fuck.

"How's working in the garage?" she asks, changing the subject and distracting me from my morose thoughts.

Breathing out, I answer, "Only been there a coupla days. I'm low on the totem pole there, but since I know my shit, the guys aren't too hard on me." At least, not yet. That's also because they're backed up, and I'm pulling them out of that. They're too appreciative at the moment to shoot a gift horse in the mouth.

"You got this, Deke."

"The job, yeah." The other shit, I'm not so sure, which is exactly why I need to talk to Cooper.

She reaches over, squeezing my hand, then gives another yawn. "Trust your mom. You are right where you need to be."

I don't answer because the door swings open, and

my father fills the frame. "How's it goin'?" he asks my mother, not once looking in my direction.

"Tired." She gives another yawn, this one bigger than the first.

"I've got it, Deke. Head on out," my father commands, coming to the end of the bed.

Just like him to take over. Whatever. I need to get to Cooper and get this shit sorted.

"No, I want him to stay," my mother tries.

"Angel, he stays, you stay awake. You know this. Best thing is for him to come back after you've had a nap."

She lets out a huge sigh. "Sorry, sweetheart."

I rise from the chair, lean over, and kiss my mother's forehead. "It's all good. I'll be back."

"Right." The word comes out a bit choked, but she keeps it together.

Looking my father square in the eye, I see his jaw jumps with a tick. I smile inside. He's pissed. Let him be. I'm done with this shit. Done.

"You wanted me, you got me," Cooper says, swinging his front door open as I walk in.

His house is a ranch-style that is covered with gray

walls and has a huge rock fireplace. There are pictures of the family all around. It's comfortable.

I'm happy for him. Happy he found what he's looking for out there. Happy he has time to spend with his Bristyl.

Time. It keeps coming back to that.

"Take a seat," he says, gesturing to one of his recliners.

"Bristyl here?"

"Nope. Just you and me. Whatcha got for me?"

His demeanor is calm and collected, reminding me so much of his father. Hell, even the way he looks is just like Uncle Cruz.

"When I left, I didn't have much of a choice."

Cooper's body gives a slight jerk, but that's all I get reaction-wise as I lay it all out—when I started using, rehab, what happened after, and the reason I left.

Cooper was the one I was closest to growing up. That was, until he reached sixteen and got his cut. Everything fell to shit then, and it was my stupid teenaged self who helped it along that path. If I could choose one man to lay this shit on, it'd be him. Back then, I was too angry. Now, well, they say age brings wisdom, and I feel that I can trust him.

When I'm done, Cooper gets up, leaves the room, and then I hear a crash, followed by a loud grunt. Hopping up from my seat, I move toward the noise.

Cooper pounded his fist through the plaster three times, causing cuts to open and blood to seep down his arm. His breathing is erratic, giving away his full outrage, but it serves no purpose.

"Not worth tearin' your house up. Your ol' lady's gonna have your balls."

His intensity comes to me, putting me on alert.

"Not worth it? Are you fucking shittin' me?" My calm and cool cousin explodes, and I feel that shit all the way down to my bones. "That motherfucker threatened our sisters, my brother, and killed someone in front of you. Not to mention doped you up to keep you in line. And he showed up last night? Motherfucker's dead," he decrees.

"Man—"

"And you," he cuts me off, the anger pouring off him. "You went four fuckin' years not here because of this shit. Because GT slammed you down, and thinkin' you had to go! Fuck that. Fuck that!" He throws his fist through the wall again, debris flittering throughout the air.

"Coop! Stop hittin' the fuckin' wall," I order. "It ain't solving shit."

Cooper straightens. "Know that. Just needed to get it out and clear my head." He takes a deep breath. "You, in your truck and meet me at the clubhouse. We're talkin' to the guys about this shit."

"Coop, I just need you at my back. We can—"

Coop enters my space, and I clench my fists. "That's not how shit works, Deke. You know this. Fucker messed with Ravage. Fucker scared a kid into leavin'. Fucker threatened Ravage kids. Fucker shows up to give you a message. Fucker will go down."

"There's no reason for my father to know any of this shit. It's over and done with. He needs to focus on my mom."

"Oh, he's gonna fuckin' know. Clubhouse. Now," he orders.

"I'm really not big on orders, Coop."

"Fuckin' do it. Deke, it's fuckin' family. We handle it as family. Clubhouse. Now." He moves to the kitchen, grabs his keys, and then we move out the door.

The clubhouse is pretty quiet when we get there, but it changes quickly as the guys show up. I nurse my beer, having that dark feeling this is going to get bad. Problem is, I don't know JK's connections or how deep he is. These guys can find that out a fuck of a lot quicker than I can.

Ravage has ways. Coop's right.

"This better be good. I was balls deep in my woman," Rhys grumbles, coming in and taking a seat in the main part of the clubhouse.

"Stop your bitchin'. Know you didn't stop until you were done," Tug throws in with a smile.

Only then does Rhys give a soft smile. "Hell yeah. Still, I could be balls deep again."

My father walks through the door. One look at me, and his jaw grows tight. Wish I knew the moment when he started hating me—if it was the first time I doped up, the second stint in rehab, or if it was before any of that even happened. Was it just because I was me, and not the me he wanted me to be?

It's like a dagger to the heart, cutting through to my soul. I thought I was over it—the disgust that comes from him—but seeing his reaction to me just adds salt to the already open, gaping wound.

"See we've got company, so must not be club business," my father says, going up to the bar and grabbing a beer before taking a seat.

This crawls under my skin, but I don't let it show. Cooper, though, he glowers at my father.

That shit isn't going to make anything better. He really needs to chill the fuck out with it. Whatever way this rolls, it's not going to be pretty.

"Good morning!" Nox calls, walking in the door with a wide smile on his face. He's a mini version of Cooper, only with a bit darker hair. Must get that from his mother.

"It's afternoon, fuckwad," Dagger calls out to chuckles.

Nox laughs. "Don't give a fuck. Had a hell of an orgasm and ready to start this fuckin' day." He looks around the room, his eyes landing on me. "What do we have here?"

"Meeting. Now sit the fuck down," Cooper chides his brother.

More men follow in. Jacks, Green, and then there's Ryker. Jacks and Green were around when I was here four years ago. They weren't patched at the time, and seeing them with their cuts now reminds me of so much I've missed.

"Aw, did you come to kiss and make up?" Ryker starts as I rise from my stool.

Austyn says the baby wasn't his, but I'm not sure if I can believe it. The way he fucking looks at her, always having her in sight when she's around. Then, when she's not, he's fucking anything and everything that moves.

"Heard you tapped that fine piece."

"Call her a piece again, motherfucker, and I'll show you."

"Testy." He turns to the guys. "Must not have gotten laid this mornin'."

"Woke up with Rylie's mouth around my cock, so I'm good thanks. How's Austyn?"

The room becomes electrified at my question, all attention coming to us.

Ryker's nostrils flare. The man has tattoos on every inch of his body, at least that's visible. Except for his face. That's the only off limits for him, I guess.

He steps into my space. "Fuckin' put a lock on that shit."

Inside, I smile. "Fuckin' stay away from my woman."

"And what're you gonna do about it?"

Cooper presses between us, pushing us away from each other. "Fuckers, this is not what this is for. Take a fuckin' seat."

"Care to tell us why we dragged our asses here?" Cruz asks before taking a pull off his bottle, then setting it down on the table.

I move back to my stool and look among all the brothers of the Ravage MC. This was supposed to be my life—sitting with them, having a beer, feeling like I belonged to something bigger. Fuck, that I even had a family instead of going at it alone.

Life is life, and too much time has already been wasted thinking about this shit.

"JK Bridges." I watch as faces contort at the man's name. "He needs to be shut down," Cooper continues. "Asshole has a death sentence and needs to meet the reaper."

"Care to explain," Cruz orders.

Cooper looks at me. "Gotta let it ride."

"Saw JK last night at the fight club Rylie works at, Schade's place. He was makin' it known that he knows I'm in town. He doesn't want me here; therefore, he's going to be trouble."

"Everything around you is trouble," my father comments.

I say nothing. However, the anger builds. The demons come out of the dark recesses of my mind as the fight inside grows, climbs, and claws its way to the surface. The urge to fight hits hard, but I tap it down, needing to focus.

Cruz rises from his chair, crossing his arms. "Best you start at the beginning."

Giving a nod, I do my best to keep my gaze away from my father. I don't want to know his thoughts on it or feelings. He doesn't get that from me. Not now.

"After the second stint in rehab, I went out. Saw JK murder a kid. He beat me, drugged me, and told me that, if I didn't leave at eighteen, he'd hook my sister, Austyn, and Nox on the strong shit, by force if necessary."

"What the fuck?" Nox growls, pushing off the wall. "He did what?"

"Everyone, calm your shit. There's a lot here that needs to be processed. Everyone gettin' pissed off before it comes out isn't going to help," Cooper, ever the diplomat, puts in, and the guys take a reprieve. I know it won't last long.

"Why the fuck didn't you tell someone?" Cruz bellows, his brows knitting.

As much as I don't want to, my gaze goes to my father. "I did. Went to my father. He assumed I relapsed. He had some words for me and didn't leave me much choice." I watch as his face jumps, but turn away to avoid any other reaction. "That's why I started fighting with Princess and got the hell out of here as soon as I could."

"Why didn't you come to me?" Cruz asks.

I shrug. "Young, stupid, and my father didn't believe me, so why would any of you?" I heave in a tight breath, wanting to look at my father and see his reaction to my words. Still, I refrain, not wanting to see his reaction—whatever it may be.

"Holy fuckin' shit," Tug says, putting his hands through his hair and looking up at the ceiling.

"Look, the point is, JK knows I'm back. I don't know what power he has around here, so I can't judge his nonverbal threat. Personally, I can beat the hell out of him and snap his neck, but there's a chance he can go after someone else. That, I'm not having." I take a pull from my beer, and then simply hold the bottle. The coolness feels good against my skin.

My father charges at me, fury bubbling off him, but this is nothing new, unfortunately. "You mean to tell me that you stayed away for four years, not tellin' a soul that this dickhead was around and could dope up your family!"

I rise, meeting him eye-to-eye. "Yep."

The swing comes hard and fast. I don't bother

ducking. No, I take it at full force, my eyes staying glued to the man who raised me.

He heaves in and out, spittle coming out from between his lips. It takes serious control on my part when everything inside of me is telling me to swing back. Everything is telling me to knock him down on his ass and show him I don't take any shit from anyone anymore. I just stare at him, dead center in the eyes, even as I feel a trickle of blood slip down my chin.

"I'm giving you that one hit, old man. You won't get a second."

"I can't believe you!" he roars, unresponsive to my warning. "What if he would've gotten Emery hooked on that shit!"

"He didn't," I respond, much calmer than I intend, which I'm proud of. "When exactly did you start hating me?"

My father flinches like I hit him, just as he did me.

"Sure, I've fucked up, but it started before then, and you know it. I'm not perfect like Cooper."

"We're talkin' about you puttin' your family in danger!" my father yells, shaking his head.

Cruz sets his hand on my father's shoulder. "No, man, we're talkin' about a kid who left, thinkin' it was the only choice he had to protect those he gave a shit about." His gaze comes to me. "You keep in check with Emery; know what's going on with them?"

I nod.

"So, you made your sacrifice and kept your pulse on family, all while makin' a life and a name for yourself alone?"

I make no motions and don't speak. Whatever they want to think or believe is on them.

Cruz flexes his hand on my father's shoulder. "Right now, we need to focus on what's going on. GT, you and I'll talk after this." Cruz releases him then turns to the brothers. "Alright, all intel on this asshole. I want to know where he shits, eats, and who he fucks. He picks his fuckin' nose, I want to know. This man, and whoever works for him, are a threat. You lock down your kids. They stay at home or you bring them here until we work shit out." Cruz turns to me. "You work with Cooper and Nox. They'll show you where to start."

Chairs scrape on the floor as men move throughout. My father finally turns and makes his way down the hallway, following Cruz.

Nox's look is one of bafflement, which we don't have time for.

This club, the one that I've tried so hard to distance myself from over the last four years, is taking my back. At my word. No qualms. Believing me and trusting me. Something I didn't feel like I'd have all that time ago.

Unlike my father, who still hasn't said a word to me. Not even a fuck you, you're full of shit. Nothing.

I hate it. Full-out hate it. It feeds the beast inside of

me. The urge to fight hits hard, but seeing the men around me, the ones who have my back, the intensity dies down. I've lived many years with only myself to take my back. Now these men are, and it's something I never thought I'd have. I find that I like it. A lot.

"Let's do this," Cooper says, and then we get down to doing what Ravage does.

CHAPTER EIGHTEEN
Rylie

CLEANING MY HOUSE HAS NEVER BEEN SOMETHING I enjoy. It's just going to get messy again, so what's the point? However, I have nervous energy. Deke called and is going to face some of his demons with his family today, and hopefully lay them to rest. Not to mention hopefully make this JK asshole go away.

I can't imagine what he feels like. It was so hard for him to open up to me, yet he did it. With his father there at this meeting, Lord knows what sparks will fly. I don't want that for him. Not that he can't handle it, but he's lived through enough guilt. He needs to be free of it once and for all. It's what we all want—to live free.

It's my day off from both places, and I wish I had to work. I need something else to do besides clean the damn house.

Brewer joins me, wagging his tail and following me

throughout the house. Although, he likes his naps on the way, obviously not having the nervous energy I do.

After taking the laundry to the washer and starting it, I move out into the living room, noting not much needs to be done. That's both good and bad.

I called Breelyn, Skyler, and Avery, hoping to get my mind off everything. It helped for a moment. As soon as I was off the phone, though, the energy was back. We plan to have a girls' night on the first night we all get off work.

X has been good, and so has Schade's. Yes, Schade was a little pissed off at me for just leaving and gave me shit for it, but he's over it, and now we're good. Princess runs a tight ship, and I'm finding myself liking it there, too.

Loud pops surround me. Glass shatters and falls to the carpet. Fear takes over as I fall to the ground. More shots. Gunshots. At my house. Crashing through windows, walls, and through furniture.

Brewer barks. I feel his hard body on top of mine. It doesn't even register that my dog is protecting me.

It takes me a moment as my house gets blown up around me before I get out from under Brewer, crawl over to the gun cabinet, and pull out my piece.

Darting to the bedroom, Brewer right beside me, I look out the window and see a lone black car, windows tinted and plates covered. Both the passenger side front and back windows are open, and two assholes, whose faces are covered, are shooting up my house.

Fuck!

As I lift my gun to take a shot, they drive off, squealing their tires down the road.

It's not until I see their taillights brake as the car turns that it hits me.

A drive-by.

Holy shit. A drive-by shooting. Exactly like what happened to my parents.

My insides seize at that thought as a fear I haven't felt in years takes over. I rush to find my phone, dialing the one person I need.

"In the middle of somethin'," Deke answers on the second ring.

"Drive-by. I'm fine, but they blew my house up," I get out, my voice not having its usual strength.

I bend down and give Brewer a rub, trying to calm him from the action and looking him over to make sure he's not hurt. Thank Christ, he's not.

"Fuck." I hear some muffles on the other side of the phone. "Be there in ten. Are they gone?"

"Yeah."

"Do you have your gun?"

I look down at the silver in my hand, the weight of it giving me little comfort. "Yeah."

"Baby, breathe. I'll be there in ten." He disconnects

as I fall to the floor by my bed, my emotions taking over.

My parents died in my childhood home. Assholes shot up the house when I wasn't there. Killed them both. They were in the kitchen, which was a direct aim from the road, and were hit several times.

Now my house. Shot up.

I try to stop the thoughts, but they whirl around like a cyclone. I rest my head on my knees, willing them to go away.

Brewer lays his head in my lap as everything comes crashing down at once. Why me? Why this? Haven't I suffered enough, living without my parents after such a heinous act? Why repeat it?

It feels like forever before Deke charges into the bedroom, scoops me up in his arms, and places me on the bed.

Brewer barks at him, but one command, and my dog listens to him.

Before I can say anything, Deke's inspecting me, roaming his hands up and down my body.

"Clean," he calls out, and then I see a few of the Ravage MC men come into the room.

Once again, Brewer barks, coming to my side. Deke leans down, rubbing him and telling him to chill. Brewer once again listens.

"I didn't get hit," I croak out. "They drove off. Black,

four-door Chevrolet Impala, blacked out windows and plates. Both passenger windows open, shooting out. Black masks, but their hands weren't covered. Both Caucasian."

"Damn, baby," Deke says, impressed, as Cruz stands in the doorway, taking it all in.

Coming up behind Cruz is GT, Deke's father. I have no clue what went down, but him being here should be a good sign. Or maybe it's just me keeping up hope. Hope that this shit will be done.

"My ... parents, they had a drive-by."

Deke cradles me in his arms. "Know that, babe. I'll get you out of here, and then figure out what the fuck this is." Deke looks at Coop, who nods his head once. "Get anything you don't want to see destroyed together. We're going to the clubhouse."

This surprises me, but I shake it off, nod, and pull out a bag. I hear the guys going through each room. Me, I throw in clothes and shoes, stuffing it as full as possible. Grabbing another bag, I throw in my bathroom crap. Then I finally move to my closet, pulling down the worn and torn shoebox. It's the only thing I have left of my parents. I tuck it under my arm, grab some cash, my gun and bullets, and head out into the living room.

"Comin' to stay with me, sweet thing?" Ryker says, and then Deke is there, hand at Ryker's throat. Ryker just smiles. "What can I say? Women love me."

"Only woman you've gotta worry about is Austyn.

Remember that." Deke pushes off Ryker, grabs both my bags, and hauls them out of the house, then he comes back, Brewer following him the entire time.

I watch as my Harley is loaded into the back of a box truck by Jacks and Green. Deke tosses them the keys to my Jeep, and they hook it up to the hitch on the back. Guess I don't have to worry about my vehicles.

"Nothin' fancy with the bullets," GT says, holding one in his hand. "Dime a dozen. We'll get the feed from the streets around the house pulled."

Just then, sirens are heard in the distance.

"Clear out," Cruz orders, and everyone piles out. "Deke, bring her to the clubhouse. You two can camp downstairs."

Deke nods.

"You don't want the cops in this?" I ask him as he helps me in the truck.

He doesn't answer until he comes around and gets in. "No. They'll contact you. You say you weren't home. They'll want to do a report, but you won't know shit because you weren't there. You have no enemies. They'll let it ride."

"Got it." I rest my head back on the seat as we pass the cops heading toward my house, Brewer sitting at my feet. Someone must have heard the shots. Still, it took Deke ten minutes to get to me.

The drive doesn't register, neither does going into the clubhouse, down the stairs, into a room, or even

Brewer's paw steps. Not until the door clicks shuts does my attention catch.

Deke's concerned gaze comes to me, and I don't think. I race to him and burrow my head into his chest as he wraps his arms around my body.

"You're okay, Ry," he assures, lifting me and holding me in his arms as he sits on the bed. "Give me all those trembles."

I do. The fear of my parents going out like that, their last breaths, their last thoughts when it was going down—it all bombards me in a rush, and I have no choice but to give it to Deke. All of it. He's such a rock, taking in everything I give him.

Brewer whines as he lies down, letting me give all of this to Deke.

"I'm gonna make this okay for you, Rylie. I swear it."

I nod absently, hearing him, but unsure of many things right now. This isn't me. This weak, trembling woman. I've always been strong. The only time I wasn't was when my parents died.

It feels like hours later, but probably is only minutes, when Deke asks me to recall exactly what happened to me—sounds I heard, thoughts I had. I relive it all. It's easier wrapped in his strength. Having someone to lean on when I haven't had that in so many years. He takes it and holds me tighter, giving me everything.

My body begins to calm and feelings start to recede.

"I'm okay, Deke. Thank you," I whisper into his shirt.

Brewer sneezes from the floor, but doesn't move.

Deke massages my back, comforting and relaxing me. "Good. Glad to hear it. I need to get upstairs and find out what's going on. Need to get in the loop about this and JK. I'll send Princess down here to stay with you. I'll be back in a bit."

"Right." I can't fall apart now; there's shit to sort.

Pulling deep within myself, I finally find what I was searching for—the tough bitch who doesn't let anything get her down. Nor will this. We'll find out who this is and take care of it.

"Sounds good. Let me know what you need me to do."

He pulls away and kisses my lips. "There's my strong girl. This shit will be sorted." He kisses me again, plants my ass on the bed, and then disappears. And surprisingly, after all the shit that happened, I don't feel the fear anymore. I feel the anger.

My mind spinning, I call Charlie, then my friends, wondering if they've heard about the shooting. None of them are happy.

CHAPTER NINETEEN
Deke

I'LL KILL HIM. FUCKING KILL HIM.

Buzz, a brother and computer guru, presses buttons on his computer, bringing up the car in question, tailing it to a known associate of JK's crew. It's the link. Fucker thinks he's going to get away with this shit, I've got news for him.

Fucking come at my woman, not even having the balls to come at me, man to man. Shows how big of a pussy he is.

Luckily, the Ravage MC know some of the police department and were able to get the delay to Rylie's house. Not that I told her that. She's not in a place for that right now.

"We don't have sound, but we have visual," Buzz says, pointing to a screen off to the left.

The car pulls into an open bayed garage. The

view then moves to inside where the men exit the vehicle. A man with his back to the camera lifts a gun and plucks off all four guys with precise accuracy.

"Fucking hell," Cruz clips. "At least we don't have to deal with them."

"Collateral. He's cleanin' up as he goes. No more leftovers like me," I tell the room and hear grunts of approval.

"Right. JK is at his place with strong guards around it."

Buzz gives us another visual, and we see JK lounging by the pool, drink in hand, a woman next to him. Sure enough, his two-story home is surrounded with men.

"Got markers. I'll call 'em in," Cruz calls out, putting his phone to his ear and walking out of the room.

"Where's Emery?" I ask my father, saying anything to him directly for the first time.

"Home with your mother."

I fully turn toward him. "Don't you think you need to get them here? This fucker just shot up my woman's home. You don't think he's gonna try your house next?"

"She's sick, Deke."

"No shit," I clip, really wanting to knock a few licks into him. "Get her out of there and here. Just in case."

My father stares at me, and for the first time in

forever, he relents, taking away his eye contact and moving to his phone.

"What about the rest of the kids?" I ask the room at large.

"Calls are going out now. Expect them here within twenty," Cooper calls out.

"Austyn?"

"Yep, called her personally. She'll be here."

A small bit of weight lifts, but I want my mom and sister here asap.

Buzz takes us through the lay of the house, noting things we may get stuck in or places that are secret. Fucker has an entire compound.

Calls are made, and people start showing up at the clubhouse, including my mother and sister. Only when I see them do I let out a sigh of relief.

JK has left the pool area, and Buzz hasn't been able to get visual on him, but we know he hasn't left the place.

My body thumps, waiting for the go-ahead to tear this man apart. No more living with him over my head. No more him giving that poison to kids and having them go through what I did. No more of him.

"Meeting," Cruz calls into the room, and we make our way to the basement in the wide-open space down there that's next to Buzz's computer area.

We move into the room as one, something that doesn't quite register.

"First thing's first." Cruz grabs something from the back of the couch and holds it up in the air.

Leather.

"Deke, come put this on," he orders, causing my throat to close up.

A cut. He wants me to put on a prospect cut. Fuck me.

I stand there paralyzed for a moment, unable to think, unable to move, unable to do anything.

The one thing I desired so damn badly is now within my grasp.

"Boy," Dagger calls out, snapping me out of my surprise. "Get your ass up there."

"Want you to be in on this. You're one of us. We don't do shit with outsiders," Cruz says, and I feel the eyes all around me, but it's my father's that I meet.

When he lifts his chin, something inside me settles in a profound way.

Not only will I be part of this operation, by taking this cut, I'll be committed to Sumner, the one place that I said I wouldn't go back to. There's no going back from this. The only out is death.

The acceptance around me, though, fills a part inside that I thought would never get filled. Never thought it would be an option. I put this leather on my back, I'm in.

The weight of the material settles on your shoulders. You carry the weight of the club with those colors. The rag, the single garment that means everything: family, loyalty, freedom.

While I wanted this for so much of my time growing up, now seeing that leather, it's more. It's not a desire to be like my father or uncle. It's being my own man, knowing what I want out of life, and knowing these men will take my back, no matter what, as I will do for them.

Being angry for so long changed a part of me, and not in a good way. I know that, and I dealt with life the way I could. If I made different choices, went to someone else, I more than likely would've never left. Never grown into the man I am today. The one who deserves that cut.

I nod, feeling a peace surround me and allowing it to come in.

"Prospect, you're in for the most grueling year of your life," Cruz says, then chuckles are heard throughout the room.

I slip on the leather, the weight heavy in a way that doesn't feel like a problem, but a solution. Damn.

Cruz slaps my shoulders. "Alright, now let's get to business."

I move through the guys, back to my place, getting hand pats as I move. This easy? This fucking easy, and I'm in the fold? Knew working at the garage would put me in with the Ravage MC, but to actually have the cut on my back is unreal.

"Alright, we've got the Vipers Creed and Ruthless Rebels on their way. Luckily, they're in the neighborhood. Okay, not quite, but they will be in the next hour, guaranteed. Buzz, we need all entry and exit points in the house. Tug and Breaker, we need eyes everywhere around the place. Jacks and Green, need weapons locked and loaded. Dagger and Rhys, get ready for retribution. No one touches the Ravage MC. No one threatens our kids. No one takes from us," Cruz states. "You've got one hour, then meet back here."

The guys leave, yet I stay rooted to the spot, leaving Cooper, Nox, Cruz, Ryker, and my father in the room.

"We got a lot of shit to work out, Deke. Know this. But we're not going to let it get in the way of what we need to do. JK needs to be extinguished," Cruz says.

Princess races into the room. "Have you heard from Austyn?" she asks all of us.

"Talked her about thirty minutes ago, Mom. She's on her way," Cooper calls out.

"She's not answering her phone. Not here. Tried tracking her. The car and phone are still at her house. Something's wrong."

"Fuck!" Cruz clips. "All of us, to Austyn's house now. Deke, you drive the truck with Nox and Cooper in case we need more fire power."

I haven't taken orders in four years, but now, it just comes natural when it comes from Cruz. I'm not sure how I'd feel if it were my father. This, however, feels right.

"Let's fucking go!" Ryker calls out, pain written all over his face. About fucking time he gets his head out of his ass.

We leave the room, and I make my way into Rylie's room.

Panic in her eyes, she tells me, "They can't find Austyn."

I pull her close. "Know that, babe. Goin' to look for her. Need you to stay here. Don't leave for any reason at all."

"You're wearing leather," she comments instead of answering.

"Another time." I lean down and kiss her hard.

Meeting the guys outside, we then head over to Austyn's house.

When we get there, she's nowhere to be found.

The pit of my stomach hollows out, and I feel my body jerk, remembering the woman who came to me, strong as can be, after doing something that proved hard for her. Strong, independent. There's no struggle, so whatever happened had to come as a shock.

We have to find her. Now.

CHAPTER TWENTY
Austyn

HIGH.

Flying.

Soaring.

My eyesight is hazy, like there is a fog over it. I'm unable to see ten feet in front of me. Sounds of movement are all around me, though, along with murmurs from a stern voice.

That voice.

I remember it.

I hear it in my nightmares. The ones that were only tamed when Deke stayed at my house.

I desperately have to get out of here, far away from him. However, my arms feel like hundred pound weights, yet light at the same time. I go to move them, but they don't want to. It's the same story with my legs and torso.

Blinking, I try to make sense of where I am and what exactly is going on.

When I left my apartment, I looked everywhere around me before exiting. I didn't expect a Taser to come shooting from a distance and knock me on my ass. He injected me with something, probably the same thing as last time that made my limbs go weak, then my mind.

Last time ...

Panic fills me at just the thought, as the memories bombard me, ones I want to forget and move past.

This doesn't bode well for me. I barely got away before. I didn't even think I'd ever be able to stand on my own two feet again. This time will be worse. I know it. He's evil. Beyond evil.

Cooper told me to get right to the clubhouse. He warned the brothers would notice if I'm not there. They have to because, for once, no amount of the brute strength force my mother taught me is going to help. Not when my body is uncontrollable, and my brain is as high as a kite.

My head jerks from a powerful force, maybe a hand. There are no cries or tears. I don't feel the pain, only a slight sting and the movement. The drugs he gave me must be more powerful than before, because I felt everything last time. Remembered everything. The brutality, the tearing, the burning—everything.

"You fucking little cunt. Get rid of my baby. Now I get rid of you."

Fear slices through me. I try to move my arms and legs to get away, but it's no use.

He pulls my hair so hard my neck angles down in an unusual way. Again, no pain, only pressure.

"Know it was mine. The other three, I made them use condoms. Not me. When I pushed through that virgin barrier, I wanted you filled with only me. Wanted you to remember who you belonged to. Then I find out you killed my baby!" The pressure becomes more, and now I do cry out. "Had my guys track you and found you after you murdered my baby! Bitch, you're going to pay ... every fucking way possible."

Bile rises up my throat, burning as I try to push it down. This man hurt me in more ways than just physical, and I hate him. Hate what he and his men did to me. I can still feel the pain of when he took me, can still feel the guys holding me down by my arms and legs while I screamed out, trying to fight back. Every damn detail of what he did to me is etched on my soul for eternity.

My baby. I fight back the tears thinking of the life that grew inside of me for such a short time.

Pain spears through my heart, and the emptiness I feel in my stomach grows.

Innocent. I can't fight the tears as one falls out of the corner of my eye and rolls down my cheek.

A sharp pain comes to my side, and then wetness falls from my body.

"Shouldn't have givin' you so much. Want you to feel this."

"Please don't, JK," I whisper, just as another slice of pain comes. Then another. And another.

It would be better if I were dead.

CHAPTER TWENTY-ONE
Deke

"Right," Cooper says into the phone then hangs it up. "Footage outside Austyn's house shows her getting tasered. Two men carrying her off, the car leading right to JK's place."

"You're fuckin' shittin' me," I growl.

"We're pullin' off. Need to brief Dad and GT."

We pull off to the side of the road and get out, relaying the information.

The guilt weighs heavily on me. I brought this to them. Fuck, I brought this to her.

"Knock that shit off right now. He's doin' this, not you," my father says, surprising me.

He's blamed me for so long that this is unreal to me. Him not thinking this is my fault. That I didn't lead all of this shit to the door of my family, even though it's the last thing I ever wanted. And he doesn't blame me? I can't help wondering: *what changed? Why now?*

I told him everything. He knows I didn't just walk out on my family, that I had reasons. That's what changed.

I only nod, unable to say anything else. I don't feel the nod one bit. It's been so long since my father said anything remotely positive to me that it seeps down into my soul, feeding that empty place that's been there for years.

Cruz starts making calls, rerouting all the other MCs to JK's place.

Ryker runs his hand through his hair, looking up at the sky. "This isn't fuckin' happenin'," he says to whoever's up above. There's no way to respond to it, but he repeats it over and over again.

"We go in hot once they get here—all of us. We go in and get my girl. Don't give a fuck who we take out, just make sure it isn't you or the guys takin' our backs. Brothers are all on their way," Cruz orders, hopping onto his bike and moving.

As much as the guilt rides me, I push it down, needing to focus on what needs to be done to get Austyn away from that fucker. Knowing what he did to me, I hate to even think what he could be doing to her.

We set up post outside the place. Buzz shows up a few minutes behind us with computer equipment that he, Tug, and his twin, Breaker, are linking up. Bikes start rolling in from other clubs, none of who I know, so I stay back and let them do their thing.

My hands twitch to get in there. Ryker is about ready to come out of his skin with each second that ticks by. Cruz, Cooper, and Nox are keeping a leash on it, but barely. Nox is close to the breaking point. I did catch myself twice going up to him, putting my hand on his shoulder, and giving it a squeeze.

He was fine with this and seemed to let out a breath every time. It's a start at least.

"Go time. In hot; take out everyone. No survivors. We'll do clean up after," Cruz orders.

We move hard and fast. The land the house is on is vast with guards everywhere. Nox and I take out two, while Cooper and Ryker take out the others. The trees around the place give good cover, keeping us on serious alert. Buzz is at the computer, watching the cameras to give us information, but that won't do us much good if it's a sneak attack.

Several other guys come onto our path, but we're able to neutralize them.

There's no doubt the place knows they're under fire, unless they're underground because of the bullets flying. Therefore, we need to move fast.

I look at my phone that has a map of the place that Buzz sent to all of us. We have the lower left quad, so we make our way there.

The walls are stucco, which makes the light shine

off them—not conducive to this ambush—but we make it work.

Not looking to see if people have a gun or not, we take them out, knowing that if we miss just one, we could be finished. The females from earlier on the cameras are nowhere in sight, only men with guns. JK's army.

I hear shots off in the distance and hope like hell they're ours.

Cooper leads us down a corridor, and we end up taking out four more men. Ryker and Nox take turns opening doors, while I take their backs and keep a lookout behind us.

This, being in the fold with these men, knowing they have my back as much as I have theirs, this is family. Having the cut on my back, being with the guys who will one day be my brothers. Being in the fold, where I wanted to be, only not for this reason.

Three more men go down by my hand. I don't give the least bit of fuck.

"Locked!" Cooper calls out, causing the hair on the back of my neck to rise.

Ryker doesn't wait. He kicks the door hard, splintering it as it crashes open. More shots, and then Nox calls out in pain.

"Graze!" he yells, still shooting.

As I make my way into the room, my stomach twists at the sight before me. Austyn's arms are tied above her head, and her legs are attached by ropes to pegs in the floor. Her body hangs limply as blood oozes out of her sides. The way the blood is stained, it looks as though she was lying down at one time. Fuck, what did they do to her?

"Help," she croaks out. As lethargic as she is, either she lost a fuck lot of blood, or he doped her up.

Two men off to the side set off shots. Pain slices through my shoulder, the burning fierce, but I aim and take one of the assholes out. Cooper takes the other as Ryker runs up to Austyn, pulling a knife out of his pocket and cutting the rope from Austyn's arms.

Moving closer, I see Austyn's face is torn up. She is covered in cuts, blood, and it looks like her nose is broken. Red and purple marks mar her face. It all causes the anger to burn inside me, especially because there's no JK in sight.

"You got her? I'm goin' to find that fucker," I growl, hearing Austyn whimper in Ryker's arms.

"I'm in," Cooper calls out, just as his phone rings.

He swipes it. "Yeah?" His eyes grow round. "Everyone out! Bomb!"

Ryker takes off like a shot. Nox is behind him, but limping. Cooper scoops him up in a fireman's hold as we run with everything we have, going through the same corridors as before, anger pumping through me and wanting to escape.

The sunlight hits us, and everything explodes.

CHAPTER TWENTY-TWO
Rylie

"You do realize you were shot, right?" Anger bubbles at my man who won't stay the fuck down.

"Three days ago, Rylie. I'm good."

Even though the doc said he'd be fine, I still don't like it. Funny how I saw him fight like hell and get busted up, yet a bullet wound to my man ... No, not liking that one little bit. Only a few inches over and it would have hit his heart. I'd be visiting his damn grave, just like my parents.

"Need to go talk to Austyn."

Placing my hand on his shoulder, I gentle my voice. "She's still not seeing anyone, except her mom and dad. They have her barricaded at their house, recovering."

The woman had multiple stab wounds; two that punctured organs that needed to be stitched up. She had blood transfusions and had to have the drugs pumped from her body. Surprisingly, they didn't keep her in the hospital long. Princess and Cruz took her home, and now she refuses to see anyone. It's been said that Ryker is camped out on their porch, and even with Cruz telling him to go home, he hasn't budged.

To me, this is quite interesting. Ryker, the man who talked about getting into my panties the first time we met, didn't seem to have a soft spot for anyone. But he does her. It's not my business, but with being around the club the past few days, word gets around fast.

"They'll let me see her."

"Why don't you go see your mom upstairs? She didn't want to leave until you were feeling better."

That woman comes off as a soft person, but damn, when she heard her boy was shot, she turned into a lioness, ready to rip anyone and everyone apart. Took everything out of her, and she ended up passing out. But damn, it was fierce.

"Fuck, I hate that she's doin' chemo, then hangin' out here."

"Babe, do you really think she's gonna leave you?"

Deke rolls his neck side to side. "Fuck."

He gets up from the bed we've been sharing. I've tried to lie on the edge, giving him more room with his shoulder, but he always pulls me to him so my head rests on his chest.

We've been staying at the clubhouse because JK got

away. Deke didn't give me all the details, just said we had to stay at the clubhouse for a while, that it was safer. I'm down with safe. Lord knows I don't need knives inside my body.

"Come on; let's go up and see Mom."

Brewer barks as we leave him in the room and shut the door. He's made quite a home here in the clubhouse. He loves to run outside in the open areas.

Entering the room, Emery runs up to her brother and wraps her arms around him. His back gives a slight jolt in pain, but he gives nothing else away as he wraps his good arm around his sister.

She's so small against him. I love seeing how much they love each other. Deke deserves this. Deserves his family.

"I'm fine. Everyone's fine," he tells her, rubbing her back.

"Austyn," she croaks out, her body shaking.

Casey, otherwise known as Angel, sits on the bed with tears in her eyes, watching her two children. I move away from Deke and go to her.

"Are you okay?"

She reaches over and grabs my hand. Her grip isn't very strong, and her face looks as if she's aged years in the past week. The chemo is doing a number on her.

"All things considered, wonderful. Got my two babies in the same room and his woman. Only thing better would be my man here. It's great."

This woman's strength is admirable. In the face of odds, all she sees are the positives of having her kids together. I'm happy that she has that.

Deke moves to the side of the bed with his sister tucked under his arm. "Wish you could go home and recover, Ma."

"This is home, Deke. Anywhere my kids and family are, is home."

My heart hurts at remembering my parents. They loved me, cared for me, and their time was cut short. Deke is getting his time back. So, while I hurt for my loss, I'm also happy for my man.

"JK and his crew are off radar," Deke tells me, which is something I've been dreading. "Talked to Cruz. He's sending everyone home. Can stay here if we want, but JK hasn't shown up in a week and a half now, and Buzz has every computer program running to find him. From what he's found so far, we know he left the state."

"Considering I've been off work for the last ten days, I really need to get back to my life, Deke. Schade's been cool, but I need to get back. Princess has been good, too, with you shot and all. Still, it's time to get back to life."

He pulls me tightly to his warm, hard, naked body.

"Gun on you all the time. You go nowhere without letting me know where you are, and I take you to work and pick you up."

I begin to refuse, but he squeezes me harder. "You're my woman; I protect you. Gotta give me this or I'll have to tie your ass to the bed."

A smile lifts my lips. "For a little while. I'm not big on being told what to do, Deke. You know this."

"But you'll do it because you know I'm keepin' you safe."

I let out a breath. "Right."

"Next, you gotta choice. You either go back to your place, clean it up, and stay there with me. Or, clean it up, sell it, and move in with me."

"You want me to move in with you?" Inside, I jump for joy like a kid on a sugar high. Holy shit, I care so damn much about this man.

"Ry, we're together every night. You haven't left my side for over a week. Fuck yeah, I want you livin' with me."

I lift my head, resting it on my hand, my cocked elbow on the mattress, and look down at my man. I want nothing more than to live with him, wake up with him, be with him. "Yeah."

"Yeah." He pulls me down to his lips and takes them hard yet sensually.

Deke's movements aren't frantic like our times in

the past. They are slow and meticulous. Each brush of his fingertips on the skin of my arms sends goose bumps throughout my flesh. I clutch his neck, holding him to me, afraid he could possibly move away. This connection between us in this moment can't break.

It feels too powerful. Too knowing. Too important.

He continues to take, and I continue to give, rubbing my thumbs along his jaw as we dance with our mouths in rhythm together.

He sucks on my bottom lip, watching me as he does so. Then he rests his elbows on either side of my head, enclosing me, which I love.

Lying skin to skin, his warmth infuses me. He lifts my knee and wraps it around his hip, still kissing me leisurely, like he has all the time in the world and nothing else matters.

He pulls away and looks deeply into my eyes, conveying so much without a word. Then Deke rubs his nose along mine, and I close my eyes, enjoying the small gesture.

"Want you raw, skin to skin. I'm clean. You on the pill?"

"Yeah," I breathe, wanting to feel all of him, too. Just him and me. Nothing else in the world exists.

He adjusts his body, his cock right at my opening, but he doesn't press in. No, instead, he tortures me, slipping the head inside and stilling, then kissing me.

With slow, meticulous movements of his hips, he enters me inch by inch by inch. Time stays still as an unbreakable bond forms between us with each of his movements.

I don't move my hands from his neck, wanting everything this is so badly I'm afraid I could lose it if I do move. He's never given me a reason, but losing my parents marked me. Deke, I don't think I could come back from that.

I love this man.

Deke continues to lazily move in and out of me, sliding all the way out to the tip, and then back in repeatedly. He stops to watch my eyes, then kisses me once again. The burn is slow building, but the intensity is so heightened, and the roll between my legs smolders.

"Deke," I whisper, my eyes begging him to move, take me over that edge, give me what I need, what he needs, what we need.

"So fuckin' beautiful, bombshell, and fuckin' mine." Only then does his thrusts increase, but not like normal. These are still way tamed, yet no less intent on serving their purpose.

The spiraling curl hits. I dig my nails into his neck as my back arches off the bed. I feel Deke's cock grow. Then I feel it twitch as he leashes his come inside my body.

We stare into each other's eyes, knowing this was more. So much more.

"That wasn't just fucking," I breathe up at my man.

A lazy smirk comes across his lips. "No, baby, it wasn't." He drops his lips to mine again.

There isn't anywhere I'd rather be than in this man's arms.

CHAPTER TWENTY-THREE
Deke

WE WALK INTO MY CHILDHOOD HOME FOUR DAYS LATER, not feeling good vibes. Tensions are already high with the club.

The brothers have brought me into the fold as if I've belonged there all my life. Even with my shoulder, though, I've had bathroom duty and those fuckers are nasty. However, I couldn't help smiling, even as I cleaned the shit.

That's saying a lot because the mood around the club is bad. JK can't be found, and I've been helping put in new security systems in the brothers' houses. Buzz says they are state of the art, and then he gave some tech-babble that I had no clue what the fuck he was talking about.

We've been searching, too, asking around and

trying to find JK, but he's gone ghost. Full-out no trace of him whatsoever.

It's putting everyone on edge. We're all aware.

Mom's hanging in there well. Meanwhile, Cruz says we need a family meeting and that Austyn won't be in attendance. She's home with Emery, the only person besides her mom and dad she'll let see her. She won't let me in. She came to me at a very difficult time, and now she's avoiding me, along with everyone else. I'll give her time. It may be a short amount of time, but I'll give it.

"Oh, my boy!" my grandma, known as Ma in the club, says, coming up and grabbing each side of my face, pulling me down to her and kissing me on the cheek. "When they told me you were here, I made Pops start the drive back. They didn't tell me until last week, those fools, saying we were on vacation and needed it. I can't believe they let all this go down without calling us."

Ma turns and glares at my father and Cruz, but it doesn't faze them in the least.

"Good to see ya, Ma." I pull Rylie beside me. "This is my woman, Rylie."

"Oh, honey." Ma grabs Rylie, pulling her into a hug. "So happy to meet you."

"Woman, back off so I can get me some," Pops, my grandfather, says, coming up behind her. He puts his arms around me, giving me a slap on the back, then giving Rylie a hug.

It's another reminder of the things I missed. Time that I can't get back, but will do my damnedest to make up now.

"Deacon," my mother calls from the recliner in the living room.

Her beautiful hair now gone, she has a scarf around her head. Her second round of chemo is fully done, and the doctors are optimistic. She's had some tests done, so we're waiting on the results, every one of us thinking positive. That's all we can do right now.

I kneel at her side and kiss her hand. "Hey. How ya feelin'?"

She gives me a soft squeeze. "Same, baby boy."

"Ma, do I look like a baby?"

Her smile comes. I love seeing it on her. "Doesn't matter your age, you'll always be my baby boy."

"It'll never fuckin' change," Cooper says, slapping my back with a smile on his face, his woman, Bristyl, holding his hand. "They'll never stop. It's not even worth wasting your breath."

"That's right," my mother agrees on a smile.

"Alright, let's get this done so I can get back home to my girl," Cruz announces.

I take a seat on the floor, pressing my back against Mom's chair and pulling Rylie down between my legs. She rests her back against my front perfectly, like she's made to be there. Then she rests her hands on mine that are pressed against her waist.

It's strange how familiar this feels after being gone for so long. It's like I wasn't gone a day, and things are back to the way they were supposed to be. How we can go back to this so quickly, I don't know. Maybe it has to do with what we saw with Austyn, or how I took everyone's backs. I don't know, but this feeling of belonging is like nothing I've ever felt. With my woman and family, not sure what could get better. Unfortunately, I don't think it's going to last long. I have this feeling, with the way that Cruz's gaze cuts through everyone, there is going to be pain.

"Bottom line is, Austyn is shut up tight." Cruz stops, taking in a breath and wrapping his arm around Princess, pulling her tight against his side. "Deke, is there anything you can give us? Why you brought her home? Why she came to you?"

My chest feels tight, weighted, heavy. Damn, this is not a place I want to be. This is a lose-lose situation, smacking me hard in the face. I tell them, I break Austyn's confidence. I don't, I could lose theirs. Worse, this is all my fault. JK said he'd hurt her. He told me flat-out, and I still came home, making a wrong choice again.

"Because of me." The words are soft, but Rylie hears them. Her body stills in my arms.

"She doesn't blame you, Deke. We've asked," Cruz starts, obviously hearing me.

"Doesn't mean it's not my fault. I came back here, and JK did what he said he'd do. Shot up my woman's house and hurt Austyn. It's on me." The guilt weighs me down like a lead balloon. "We need to find him and make him pay."

"Baby," Rylie starts, but I move to get up, needing to walk out some of this energy.

I hoped the demons were gone, but finding out this was more than likely my fault isn't what I want to hear. The urge to get into the ring and pound some flesh hits hard.

Inside, fury takes over. I try to push it away, wondering if I would've stayed away if she wouldn't have been hurt.

Everything crashes around me, and I feel my knees begin to give. Reaching out, I grip the wall to hold myself up, the weight settling on me hard.

"Son," my father calls out, walking over to me.

We haven't had a sit down or man to man since everything came out. Not gonna lie, I haven't wanted to start it all up again. Wanted to move past it. However, it's now time to hash it out, which isn't a good thing. My emotions are too high. I've been doing a damn good job keeping my head on straight when he's around. Now, I'm not sure I can dig deep enough for that level.

"Don't weigh this shit on your shoulders. It's on mine."

I stand there in stunned silence as my father takes accountability for what happened all those years ago, something I never thought would happen in my wildest dreams. It kills me knowing everything we lost. Knowing that he pushed me away and let that eat at me for so many years.

"Shoulda listened; that's on me. Gotta carry that around for the rest of my life. Knowin' I'm the one who didn't listen when you were tryin' to do good. This shit is a result of my fuck up. One that I'll be tellin' Austyn I'm sorry for, for the rest of my life. You don't get that. You don't get that guilt. That's on me, and I'm takin' it."

My mother sobs in her chair, and I see Rylie move over to hold her hand in comfort. I thank God I have such a great woman.

"Dad." The word feels foreign because I haven't used it in so long, at least not in the way I am now, with sincerity. I feel the clog in my throat, but push it down.

"Never hated you, Deke. Just saw so much in you and knew you had so much inside that you weren't living up to. I fucked that shit up and didn't do right. I take that. It's my burden to bear. All these years, I wondered what I could've done different, and there they were, smacking me in the face every damn second."

He clears his throat before continuing, "When you

were born, your mom and I were so damn scared we were going to lose you, and I had all these ideas of what you'd be. You were on the right path for so long, and somewhere I fucked up and let you go down the wrong one. Know that now, and know I put it all on you. Not fair. I've made mistakes. I own them. Just hope you and I can heal. Son, I'm sorry."

When he clasps his hand on my shoulder, it takes everything in me to keep myself together. Never thought this day would come.

"Pissed you had to stay home because of your mom bein' sick, but happy for it nonetheless." He pulls me to him, and I crash into his chest willingly, wrapping my arms around him.

Years. For fucking years, this feeling inside of me rode me hard. Then, in one moment, with only a few words, that part of me settles. *Fuck.*

"Right. I need to get back to Austyn," Cruz says. "She's dealin' with all this shit. Won't talk to us. But she's strong, and we'll figure this shit out. She doesn't want to see Ryker, and that little shit won't leave my porch. Can one of you make sure the man eats at some point?"

My father and I break apart, giving our attention back to Cruz.

"Yeah, Dad," Nox says.

"Well, I'm making food," Ma proclaims, moving

into the kitchen. "We need to eat, and I'm good at this. Food always helps." Ma takes off, concern all over her face, as Cruz and Princess make their exit.

Everyone is feeling Austyn's pain and adjusting in their own way. Hate it, but we deal.

"Is there anything I can get ya?" Rylie asks my mother.

"Water, please."

"Of course." She moves in the same direction as Ma.

"Time has come, boys, to put this shit between the two of you in the past. You've got good women, good heads on your shoulders, and need to work through this. It's time. It's been too fuckin' long. Now, I need a beer," Pops says, leaving my father, mother, and me in the living room.

"We both fucked up. Me worse because I shoulda listened to you, instead of bein' a dick. Now we move past it and get on with our lives."

"Just like that?"

"Yeah, boy, just like that."

And that's what we do. Move the fuck on. It's something I'll never forget, but he's said his peace, admitted he was wrong, which is tough for a man like GT. Now we pick up and start to rebuild. It'll take time, but eventually, it'll happen.

"WE'RE gonna need to have a garage sale," Rylie says from the living room of my apartment. "I think we should just buy a house together."

"Fine by me."

"What?" she gasps.

"Don't like it here, but needed a roof over my head. You want a house, let's get a house. I'm good with that. Pick what you want, I'll buy it."

"We'll buy it."

I pull her to my body, and she brings her hands to my chest, clenching my shirt. "I have a dick."

"We've established this on more than one occasion."

My lips tip up. "Right. So, dick, I pay. You want shit inside the place, go for it. I pay for the house and utilities. It's not up for debate."

"Deke, I make damn good money. I want to contribute."

Brewer jumps up, giving a small grunt in agreement to Rylie.

No.

"Get that. So, you buy the shit you want for the house. That's the deal."

She glares at me in that sexy way that makes my dick hard as a rock. "So, what, this is gonna be your excuse every time you want something? You have a dick?"

"Damn right."

"You *are* a dick."

I crush my mouth to hers, intent on showing her how much she likes my dick. Her moans and mewls are the sexiest sounds I've ever heard. Well, that and her screaming my name while my dick's planted inside her.

Walking her over to the table, I spin her around and press her body down on the table.

"What are you doing?"

I grip her wrists and clutch them behind her back. "Fuckin' my woman. Showin' her exactly how much she wants my cock."

The dog barks, then whines. I pin him with a look, and he takes off to the other room. He's a damn good dog.

Reaching around, I unbutton her jeans and pull them down to her knees, along with her underwear. Her wet heat glistens in the light as I pull out my cock, rubbing it through her wetness, hearing her moan yet again.

Lining up, I thrust my cock inside her. Her pussy feels like a tight vise, gripping me, sucking me into her more and more. She tries to wiggle her hands out of my grasp, but I hold on tighter, using the leverage to thrust harder. The table moves beneath us, but I don't give a fuck if it slides totally across the floor.

"Deke!" she screams as her walls close in, pulling the orgasm from my body.

Fuck, this woman undoes me.

CHAPTER TWENTY-FOUR
Rylie

SCHADE'S CLUB IS THUMPING TONIGHT, EVERYONE pumped for the "big fight." Schade's made a huge production of this one because it's a high-level fighter, meaning he's only lost three fights in his career. Money is high, and the energy is higher.

After the three beginning fights, the crowd is roaring, stomping their feet in the dirt and pushing people to get closer to the stage.

Once, I loved this—the rush, the hot and sweaty bodies moving in time with the fight. I even loved it when smaller altercations broke out and I put an end to them. Now, after everything that's been going on and how my life has changed, the need for this isn't there anymore. The urge to get in there and break people up these last two times has just been a job, and not one I enjoyed.

Strange how priorities change.

Deke is my number one priority now. When it happened, I have no clue. I think it was about the time he got shot. That was when I realized how much I cared about him. Then moving in together and beginning to build this life together, it's changed my perspective on several things.

Also, Deke hasn't fought since the last time I brought him here. He hasn't had that need. In turn, I haven't had it, either. It's just vanished. I, of course, do it because I have to, but I'm thinking my time here is coming to an end.

Deke's torn up about Austyn. There's nothing I can do about it but be there for him when he wants to talk about it, which isn't regular by any means. He's a good man. A great man. I do my best to remind him of that every damn day so he doesn't let the guilt I know he feels consume him.

Even though a couple of weeks have passed, I still make sure to tell Deke where I am. It gives him peace of mind, and really, it's no skin off my teeth.

The main fight takes over the room, and people go crazy. I find myself in the throng of another fight. After breaking it up, I notice Jackson across the way, his fists balled up and ready to go at it.

Getting over to him is a crush, but before I can, he's already thrown a punch at a man, sending him to the ground and knocking down a woman in very high sandals. She screeches, grabbing on to several different people and pulling them with her.

I get over to Jackson, pulling his arm behind his back. "Come on, buddy."

He fights me, so I bend his wrist back. Only then does he move in the direction I'm pushing him.

I nod at the guys on my team, letting them know I have Jackson and will toss him out on his ass. This is the shit that isn't holding my attention anymore like it used to. Don't get me wrong, I can kick ass, but I'd rather be at my man's apartment.

Definitely going to rethink my job here. X is fine, but this one is going to have to go.

"Jackson, what have you done now?" I ask, pushing him through the hallway where the noise isn't nearly as loud yet still echoes off the walls.

He gives a little pull. "That asshole tried to punch me. He needed to be taught a lesson," he growls.

I smile. "And you're just the badass motherfucker to do it, huh?"

Opening the door, I push him out of it. He gives a stumble and falls to his knees. Geeze.

I move out to help him up. "You gotta stop doin' this shit, Jackson. You're gonna end up in that ring with someone who'll take your head off."

We stand in the back alley, the night calm, except for Jackson's angry growls as he moves away from me.

A car screeches through the alley, headlights right

on Jackson. I push him out of the way just at the car swerves, hitting me hard in the hip. Fire radiates through my thigh and down my leg as I fly through the air and land on the dirt and rock covered ground. I try to save my head from hitting the ground, but it hits anyway.

Colors burst behind my eyelids as a searing pain starts right at my temple and moves to the middle of my skull, hard and intense.

The car slams to a halt. Then a door opens before I hear footsteps.

Pulling my shit together, I reach behind my back for my gun and open my eyes to see a blur. The gun is kicked from my hands.

Moving as quickly as my body will allow, which isn't fast, I try to roll away, but something hits me square in the back. I fight. With everything I have, I fight.

A man has me. I can tell by the pressure on me. I kick up, trying to meet his nuts. With my dizzy-ass not getting my bearings yet, I miss, but nail him in the thigh.

"Bitch!" he grunts.

I recognize the voice.

My head *booms*, but I'm able to get my eyes open enough to confirm.

"Lance?"

What the ever-loving fuck?

Electricity blasts through me, and I see black.

Cool water splashes on my face, waking me up. My limbs feel weak, like I touched a damn live wire. There's even a vibration through me that isn't natural.

Lance fucking stun-gunned me. I'm going to kill him.

Coming to my senses, I try to move my hands, but they're held strongly by something. Opening my eyes, panic flares. My hands are duct taped to a steering wheel, as well as my legs. I look out and see the Sumner lake in front of me; only the moon glistening off the water giving me any light.

"About time you woke up."

I shift to the window that's halfway down. "Aunt Beatrice?"

Shocked doesn't even cut what I feel.

"You dumb bitch. All you had to do was give me money. Why do you think I had your folks killed all those years ago? Money!"

Confusion bombards me as I struggle to put the pieces of this fucked up puzzle together through the haziness in my brain. Then anger, filled with hate, takes over.

"What do you mean? You killed my parents? What are you talking about?"

"Always the fast one. Doesn't matter. You die, as your only living relative, I get your shit. Done."

I tug at the tape, seeing if it has any give, which it doesn't. "You've lost your fucking mind."

"That's the great part. I lost it a long time ago." She actually smiles.

Lance comes into sight. "Can we do this shit so I can get back to the bitch in my bed?" he complains.

"Hang on, boy," Aunt CB says, thoroughly enjoying me trying to get my hands free.

I pull harder, the tape tearing at my skin. The steering wheel moves just a bit, but it's not enough.

"Seeing you drown while borrowing my car … such a travesty." She shakes her head in mock sadness.

"You really think anyone is gonna buy that shit?"

Biding time. That's what I need to do.

I look at the dash and see the time is eleven thirty-eight. Deke's been picking me up from Schade's. He'll know I'm not there. I just need to bide time.

"Doesn't matter. You forget Lance here knows a coroner? He's going to help me."

My mind scrambles. "He went to school with him, but he doesn't talk to him now."

"Shut the fuck up," Lance growls, throwing his fist across my cheek.

Not going to lie and say it doesn't burn, but I don't give him the satisfaction. I feel a twinge of blood run down my lip, but I don't bother swiping it off.

Asshole.

"Whoever pulls me out is going to see the tape on

me. Did you think of that?" These two are a bunch of idiots. No police officer is not going to put that in a report with a dead body. Please.

"That's the good part. Lance is going to go in and cut them off."

"The fuck I am," he challenges. "That wasn't the deal. I was to get her in the car. Did that. My shit is over. Give me my cash. I'm out."

I laugh at their stupidity. "You mean to tell me, you're going to put me in the lake, tied to a car, and he's going to swim down to me and take the tape off me ... in the water."

Stupid fucking morons, I tell ya. At least I know they don't know how to hide a damn body.

"You want to get paid, you'll do what I say!" Aunt CB pulls out a gun—my gun—and points it at Lance. Her hand is steady and knowing.

Alright, shit's getting real. Maybe CB isn't as stupid as I thought, but she damn sure is crazy.

"Stick your foot in, release the brake, and put it in neutral. Now!" Aunt CB yells at Lance.

He holds his hands up, fear in his eyes. What a pussy.

When he reaches in, I slam my head into his, using all my might, causing his head to hit the wheel. He cries out in pain, moving out of the car and holding his nose as blood gushes out of it.

I prepare for the strike to my face, and he doesn't

disappoint, but this time, it's two, his hand slipping on the second one from all the blood.

"You fucking bitch!" he roars.

Aunt CB puts the gun to Lance's head. "Do it," she orders.

I prepare myself to strike him again.

I pull at my feet, realizing they are taped to underneath the seat. If I remember right, this car has a lever with a side opening to it. If I could wiggle my legs out, I could get free.

"Go on the other side, you idiot!" Aunt CB yells, and Lance listens. "I'll push down the brake; you do the shifting. I don't know why I picked such a moron."

"Me, either," I grumble, waiting for the opportunity to elbow, knee, or head bunt either one of them. This time, though, they don't give it to me.

Keep a straight head.

I suck in a deep breath and run the scenario in my brain, the entire time pulling and moving my legs, trying to get free. The windows on both sides of the doors are rolled all the way down as the car begins its roll into the lake.

Holy shit. This isn't happening. This can't be fucking happening.

I pull hard, but the damn tape is too strong. So strong that all it does is rip my skin, but I don't care. If there's a chance it'll rip, I'll bear through it.

The car rolls into the water, the liquid coming up over the hood.

Panic hits. Deep-rooted panic. And no matter how much I try to keep a clear head, I know, deep down, this is my end. I'll never get to have a home with Deke. Never get to have a family with him and the Ravage MC. Never get to have a happy life after years spent in hell. Never get to maybe have babies or just live.

Tears well up in my eyes as I fight the tape, not letting a single second take me down in defeat. If they want me dead, it's going to be a fight, because I won't give up. Not until my last breath is on this planet.

The water spills over into the window as the car rolls deeper into the blackness, the moon now giving an eerie glow, but maybe that's just because my end is here.

Even when Deke finds out I'm not at work, he won't know to look for me here. He won't know that I'm in a car under the water. He won't know that I need him to help me with every fiber of my being.

The tears spill over as the water sloshes over my feet, up my calves, and to my knees. It's coming in at a rush, and fear like no other takes root.

I never thought I'd be as scared as when my parents died or when Deke was shot. However, this fear is for the future, one that I won't get to live with the man I love. A life that has been wasted.

Coldness covers me now from the waist down and

is rising quickly. The water is making it more difficult to get my legs free. It's like an added weight or pressure, restricting me. I hate it. Hate it.

Jerking back on the steering wheel, I fight, tears falling from my eyes as the water moves up to my chest, then to my chin. I tip my head up, gasping for air, but the water keeps coming like a natural spring, one that's going to take my life from everything I love.

I suck in a deep breath as I go under, pulling and thrashing, the force of each movement greatly diminishing from the water pressure.

My lungs burn, starving for oxygen, as I frantically look around, noting nothing to help me. Nothing around. Nothing.

Opening my mouth, water rushes between my lips, filling my lungs, and sucking the life from my body.

My last thought is ... *Deke, I love you.*

CHAPTER TWENTY-FIVE
Deke

I CRASH MY FIST INTO HIS JAW, MAKING HIM CRUMBLE TO the ground.

"We got it," Nox calls out, holding his phone to his ear.

Tonight, I had Nox with me when we went to pick Rylie up, because we had some work to do for the club. When I pulled up and saw an asshole freaking out in the back of Schade's place, I shook him out; found out someone knocked out my woman and took her. Thank fucking Christ we came early.

The asshole gave me the model of the car and a partial plate. Then he told me it was a man about Rylie's age with light blond hair. Part of me was relieved it wasn't JK. The other part wants to know who the fuck has my woman.

"Buzz has the car at the lake. We have to go right fucking now."

I race to my bike, throw my leg over, and then Nox and I take off like bats out of hell. It doesn't take us long to get there, but looking around, we don't see anyone there.

I turn off the bike and hop off, looking out at the water.

Bubbles come from about twenty feet from the bank.

"Don't fuckin' move!" Nox calls out, pointing his gun at a huge bush. It's then I see the glint of a gun.

Two figures walk out. The man, I have no fucking clue who he is. The woman, though …

"Where the fuck is she!" I yell, marching up to her as she aims the gun at me.

A shot goes off, and the woman screams as blood splatters my chest. Nox shot the woman's hand clear from her body.

The asshole man with her bends over and pukes right on the spot.

The aunt screams and cries as I move to the man, kicking him in the gut, not giving one shit if he pukes on me. "Where the fuck is she!"

He looks up at me, nasty shit hanging from his mouth. "Water," he groans, falling to the ground.

I look out at the water and see a couple more bubbles float up.

"Nox!" I yell, running into the water before diving under.

Everything is black. Pitch fucking black. I have to pop back up to get my breath. Fear like no other wraps around my heart, threatening to strangle everything out of me. Threatening to take me under the water with Rylie.

No, this isn't happening.

I move toward the bubbles and go under again, hearing splashes behind me and knowing Nox has my back.

I feel around blindly, hoping like hell I can find her. Needing air, though, I pop back up and turn toward Nox, who has a flashlight. *Holy shit!*

"I can't find her!"

Nox splashes in the water. "The car. There's a fuckin' car here. Find the metal," he orders.

I suck in a deep breath, nod, and then we both dive back down. The light glistens through the water.

I reach out and pray I can feel the metal. Pray it's there.

I have no idea how long she's been under. I have no idea if she's still alive. But Christ, please let her be.

She doesn't know it, but she's my fuckin' rock. I can't do this shit without her. My life won't be my life without her. *Fuck.*

My hand grazes something just as the light hits it.

A car. However, I have to pop up and grab air again. Fuck, I've come up how many times for air? *Shit!*

I go straight back down, pulling Nox with me. Metal hits my hand. The frame of a window. Hair. Fuck, hair!

Nox shines the light, and we see Rylie, her beautiful face lifeless. Nothing.

My heart breaks into a thousand pieces as I see her hands are taped. I reach to my boot and grab my knife, cutting her out while Nox holds the light. Then I pull her and find her feet taped, as well.

With thoughts of hearing Rylie laugh again, I muster all the energy I can and cut her legs from the car, then pull her up as I gasp for breath when we breach the surface.

With every bit of strength I have, I move her quickly out of the water, Nox right behind me.

Not knowing how the hell to do it, I start CPR, breathing into her body and pumping her chest with my hands.

Please be alive. Please be alive. Please be alive.

Tears fall from my eyes as I watch her with each push on her chest. She doesn't move. She doesn't react. She doesn't breathe. Even blowing into her mouth and seeing her chest rise does nothing.

I can't stop. Not when I hear the ambulance. Not when they tell me to back away. Not even when Nox grabs me under my arms and pulls me away. I try to fight him, but every bit of my soul is laying on the ground, in the dirt, having taken her last breath.

Life is cruel on so many levels. Missed years of my life without my family. Now I'll miss the rest of it without the woman I love.

My body gives out as I collapse, all the while watching two EMTs working on pumping life into my woman. Each movement only makes the pain worse.

Bikes rumble in the background, but all my attention is on my woman.

When Rylie gasps, I'm up on my feet, running toward my woman. The EMT tilts her to the side as water gushes from her lips and she gasps for breaths.

I fall to my knees, staying out of the way but close enough to her, dumbfounded, shock on my face, unable to breathe myself.

"We need to move now!" an EMT says as they load her up. He looks down at me. "Get in."

I hop up and move, not wanting to waste a single second.

I look at my woman. "Love you, Rylie. Fuckin' love you."

I PACE THE ER, back and forth, back and forth. They lost her once in the ambulance and had to pump life back into her. They talked about brain damage and all kinds of other shit, but all I could focus on were her breaths coming in and out. Nothing else could penetrate. Until now, as I pace, each step agonizing.

Brain dead.

This is exactly what I mean about life being cruel.

"What's the word?" my father asks, coming through the door, my mother attached to his side. She looks better, but she shouldn't be here. I just don't have the energy at the moment to fight it.

"Still waiting."

My mother walks up and wraps her arms around me. Everything inside of me cracks wide open, and while my mother holds me, for the first time since I was a kid, I sob.

"RYLIE HOLLISTER?"

I dart from the window, heading straight toward the gray-haired man in green scrubs. His face is somber. It scares the ever-loving shit out of me.

Pure terror consumes me as I feel my family at my back. The entire Ravage MC showed up, all here in the waiting room. All but Rhys, Dagger, and Breaker, who I'm told have the aunt and the asshole. Not that I give a flying fuck at the moment.

"Yes?"

"She has no one listed as her next of kin," he says hesitantly.

"I'm her man. I need to know she's okay."

The doc peers around at everyone in their cuts, his hand trembling. He better start talking before he ends up on his ass. My patience left a long damn time ago.

"Right." He clears his throat. "Ms. Hollister is alive. And I'll be straight with you, I don't know how. For as long as it appears she was under water, she's breathing on her own. However, we did have to shock her heart twice to bring her back."

My heart falls to my feet, and my mom grips my arm, giving me comfort.

"I'm worried about brain damage. We took her in for an MRI, and there appears to be no bleeding on the brain, which is good. But there is swelling, and some of it is significant. We've put her in an induced coma to help with the swelling, and we're pumping her full of antibiotics because pneumonia is very common in cases like these. The next twenty-four hours are critical. Unfortunately, all we can do is wait. If all her numbers stay the same, this is good. We'll do another MRI and see if there is progress on the swelling."

"Christ." I run my hand through my hair, knowing this isn't the worst news, but it's not the greatest, either. "Can I see her?"

"In about an hour. We're monitoring her very closely; you need to give us time to help her."

I turn away from the doc. "Please do."

He leaves as my family comes around me, but I push them off. I need some time, and they give me that, letting me pace. I'm not trying to be a dick to them. I just can't handle shit right now.

The door to the ER opens, and my eyes fly to it. Austyn walks in, a timid look on her face. I hear gasps because she's locked herself up tight in her parents' home. She makes not one acknowledgement of any of them, however. Instead, she comes directly to me, wraps her arms around me, and holds on tight. I reciprocate, holding on for dear life.

MACHINES *BEEP* AND *PING*, but it's the breathing machine I fucking hate. The sounds of the air going into Rylie's body, then the *tick* and *swoosh* it makes as it comes out. Over and over and over again, never stopping. Never a reprieve.

The worst part about it is how she's breathing, in a fucking coma.

The last MRI came back better. The doctor says they're going to start to bring her out of the coma. This is going to be the tell if she has brain damage. If she comes out and is responsive.

He once said the word vegetable, and it took my father holding me back from punching the guy. My beautiful woman is so full of life.

Three of her crazy ass friends came. Even Charlie and Schade made an appearance. I wasn't in the mood to talk to them, so my mother and Emery did that shit.

Nevertheless, she's loved. By so many damn people. I just need her to be able to wake up.

That's where we are now. I'm sitting, just waiting for my beautiful woman to wake up. The doc and nurses left just moments ago, taking all the damn tubes from her mouth, and are now watching her like hawks. So far, so good.

Nox comes behind me and places his hands on my shoulders. I don't tense, move—nothing. I don't have the energy to do so. Every bit of it is going to my girl. He's been here, though, only leaving me briefly, mostly sitting off to the side by the window. Here but not, giving me the support he can without being in my fucking face.

Having him by my side is much like the days when we were younger. He always had my back before I turned to the other shit. Feels good to have his back again after everything.

"Brother, do you need somethin'?"

"Her to fuckin' wake up," I reply instantly.

He squeezes my shoulder. "Know that. She will."

A lump forms in my throat. "You so sure?"

"Damn right. That woman is tough as hell. She's not ready to go yet."

I shake my head and close my eyes. "She can't be ready."

Nox comes around, momentarily stealing my attention from the bed. "She even tries it, you and I go in and get her back."

That lump gets harder to control, knowing he has mine and my woman's back. All I can do is nod as he does the same then moves off by the window again.

With each second that ticks by, more of the fear creeps in. I want to yell at her, "*Wake the fuck up*," but I know it won't do any good.

I hate it. Fucking hate this shit.

Inside, I'm empty.

PRESSURE COMES TO MY HAND, and I pop up. Relief floods me when I see my beautiful girl's green eyes and a smile on her lips.

CHAPTER TWENTY-SIX
Rylie

Two Weeks Later

I LIE ON THE COUCH IN DEKE'S APARTMENT, LOOKING UP at the ceiling. If he doesn't stop treating me like glass, I'm going to hurt him.

Brewer lies at my feet. He hasn't left me for any long period of time. He must have his doggie sense and knows that I was hurt and wants to protect me.

"I love you, but if you don't stop this shit, I'm going to plan your murder."

Deke pulls me into his lap, my most favorite place on the planet. "You love me, huh?"

Well, hell, guess I just threw that one out there, but I did have a near death experience, even if he doesn't like to bring it up because it makes him all twitchy. I get it. Of course I didn't see me, but I lived it.

"Yeah."

"Good, because I love you, too." He pulls me to his lips and kisses me softly, yet deeply and possessively.

Yeah, I love this man.

One Month Later

"You sure your mom's up for this?" I ask, flitting around Deke's parents' kitchen, putting out the food for the party that will be starting in the next thirty-five minutes. Emery's helping and Deke's supervising again, because he has a dick.

Asshole.

"She wanted it, she's gettin' it," he responds.

Angel's tests came back, and they came back good. Her remission is something for us all to celebrate. I'm not knocking that one little bit. It's just that she's still pretty weak, unable to lift things or exert too much energy at a given time. It's taken a toll on her body, yet her spirits are damn good. I have all the confidences that she's fought it for good. However, there's always that chance, and the doctors say she has to routinely get checked, but I feel good about things.

Even Deke is lighter, one less thing off his

shoulders. Anything that takes the weight off him, I'm more than happy for.

"Mom gets something in her head, it's hard to change it," Emery responds, setting a platter of cold cuts on the table. "She wants all her family around to celebrate this, so we'll give it to her."

I smile. "Right."

"How are you feelin'?" Emery asks, and I smile over at her.

"Wonderful."

Never been better is more like it.

People file in while I deal with guys wanting to start fights. Being the hostess with the mostest isn't an easy task, but I fight through it.

Luckily, my brain decided to stay with me after the near drowning. Sometimes, it takes me a few more minutes to remember something, but I can't complain. The only thing that really gets me, though, is my reflexes aren't as good. I'm working with Charlie in the gym to beef those up.

I quit Schade's place, but I still work at X, and I'm happy about it.

Bristyl, Cooper's woman, helps dole out the food and keep it filled. I realized quickly she's a kickass woman. Leah, her friend and Green's woman, also came and helped.

Laughter catches my attention. It's because it's Deke's. A deep, low rumble, but it's there.

He's here with his family, laughing. I can't ask for anything more than that, besides waking up every morning in his arms.

We were lucky in the house department. I didn't even fight him on the purchase. I just made sure the inside was nice and a home. A real home. That's what I wanted out of this. A place that we could grow. A place that reminds me of a time when my parents were alive. And a place to give us both peace. We found it.

This room filled with people who love my man, who care about me, is what life's about. My family left me because of a twisted woman. I'll never have my mother and father back, and missing them will be a daily occurrence until my last breath. But being surrounded by the Ravage MC fills a part of me that's been a void for so long.

Deke has given that to me. He has pulled me into his life through the ups and downs, continuing to stand by my side. He's given me so much, and I'll spend my life giving back to him.

CHAPTER TWENTY-SEVEN
Deke

One Week Later

RYLIE'S TITS BOUNCE UP AND DOWN AS SHE RIDES MY cock hard. I grip her hips, not needing to help her, yet unable to stop myself. She moans, grinding down on me, swiveling her hips and driving me to the brink of coming.

I flip her, taking control, pumping inside of her repeatedly as she claws at my shoulders. Then she explodes, wrapping so tightly around my cock, she milks me.

"Love you," she says breathlessly.

Every damn time she tells me this is a fucking blessing. Hearing her, feeling her, touching, tasting her —everything about her is my miracle. Time with her, I will not waste it. Ever.

Looking over at the clock, I say, "Need to get to the clubhouse."

"Thought you weren't workin' at the shop today?"

My job at Banner kicks ass. I'm back to workin' on cars, trucks, and bikes, in my element. While I liked being behind a desk sometimes, it's nice to be in the thick of things. My employment there went on and off the rails with everything that happened, but now, I'm there full-time, plus some. I wouldn't change a damn thing.

"On clean-up duty."

"Gross," she groans.

She's not wrong. Last night was a hell of a bash at the clubhouse, for no other reason than to celebrate. Prospecting for the Ravage MC has its ups and downs, and this is one of those downs, but it's part of it all.

Being in the fold is an experience all its own. The way they have my back, give themselves freely, as I do the same—it's beyond fantastic.

Each day, I gain more respect with the brothers. And each day, I wish I would've made different choices. But what's done is done.

"Right. Sooner I get shit done, the faster I can get back in bed with you."

"Okay," she replies sleepily.

Drunk sex with Rylie is top notch. We'll be replaying that many times to come.

"Bike," Cruz orders as I come out of the now sparkling clean bathroom.

Fuck, I just brought the hose in and sprayed the walls down. It was beyond disgusting. But last night was a celebration, one that I wouldn't have missed for the world.

"Why are we here?" I ask my father as we pull up to the lake, the one place on this fucking planet I never want to see again. I almost lost my woman here. Almost lost my entire life. I have no need to ever be here again.

The brothers walk to the banks, forming a line as they look out over the water.

My gut tightens, remembering the fear of not being able to get to my woman. Not being able to help her. Seeing her body lying on the ground, lifeless. All of it.

My heartbeat picks up as I take a couple of steps forward.

"They're gone. Bottom of the lake, where they fuckin' belong," my father says.

Relief floods me at knowing the two assholes who tried to take my woman are no longer on this earth.

"Know you've got a lot of shit goin' on. We get settled, big party at the clubhouse."

That right there is love. It's a type of love I thought I'd never have, yet they gave it to me.

"What's goin' on?" I ask.

Cruz just looks at me and lifts his chin to the door.

I move out of it and see the brothers all lined up. My father has a smile on his face.

"Today, we ride," Cruz says, slapping his hand on my shoulder.

When I was a kid, this is all I thought about, and now it's finally happening. Four years of hate and anger have turned into this moment. I'll put in my time as a prospect, then I'll wear the Ravage MC cut until the day I die.

I load up, head to the back of the line, and have the best fucking ride of my life.

Life is filled with decisions. Those decisions have consequences. The ones I made cost me years away from my family. It's all time I can't get back. Now, though, I live each day respecting each second I spend with them, knowing how it feels not to have it, and never wanting that again.

Finally getting in life what I desired for years—the cut, the club, family, and a rock-solid woman—there isn't anything more a man could ask for.

The end ... please consider leaving a revie

Keep reading for a Bonus...

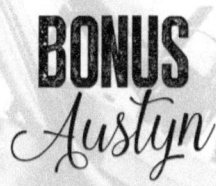

BONUS
Austyn

Guilt.

Hate.

Anger.

Fear.

All these emotions are a dangerous concoction.

Too bad every single one of them runs through my veins, just waiting to break through.

I refuse to let him win.

I refuse to be the woman I've been for the past few months.

No more.

Revenge will be mine.

ACKNOWLEDGEMENTS

Editing by: C&D Editing
   Proofread: Silla Webb
   Cover Design by: Cassy Roop at Pink Ink Designs
   Photography by: Wander Aguiar
   Models: Zack Salaun & Kali Feline

ABOUT RYAN

Ryan Michele is the *Wall Street Journal* and *USA Today* **Bestselling author** of over 40 romantic suspense novels. She found her passion bringing fictional characters to life, being in an imaginative world where anything is possible. Her knack for the **unexpected twists and turns** will have you on the edge of your seat with each page. She is best known for **her alpha, bad boy bikers and strong, independent heroines who refuse to back down.** When she's not writing, you can find her on her swing, watching the water ripple in the pond and daydreaming about her next book.

Join my Reader Group: Ryan's Sultry Sinners
Sign Up for my Newsletter

Come find me:
www.authorryanmichele.com
ryanmicheleauthor@gmail.com

facebook.com/authorryanmichele
twitter.com/Ryan_Michele
instagram.com/author_ryan_michele
BB bookbub.com/authors/ryan-michele

Thank you for reading!

Ryan
Michel